Seraphina's Circle

by

JOCELYN SHIPLEY

SUMACH PRESS

Library and Archives Canada Cataloguing in Publication

Shipley, Jocelyn,
Seraphina's circle : a young adult novel / Jocelyn Shipley.

ISBN 1-894549-51-1

I. Title.

PS8587.H563S47 2005   jC813'.6   C2005-903933-7

Edited by Rhea Tregebov
Cover & Design by Liz Martin

*Sumach Press acknowledges the support of the Canada Council
for the Arts and the Ontario Arts Council for our publishing program.
We acknowledge the financial support of the Government of Canada through
the Book Publishing Industry Development Program (BPIDP)
for our publishing activities.*

ONTARIO ARTS COUNCIL
CONSEIL DES ARTS DE L'ONTARIO

Printed and bound in Canada

Published by

SUMACH PRESS
1415 Bathurst Street #202
Toronto ON Canada M5R 3H8

sumachpress@on.aibn.com
www.sumachpress.com

for Allan

ACKNOWLEDGEMENTS

My thanks to Sumach Press, to my editors, Rhea Tregebov
and Jennifer Day, and to my husband and family, for their
constant support, insight and inspiration. Thanks also
to Halina Below and Heather Kirk, whose comments
on early drafts of this book were invaluable
in shaping the final version.

1

IT'S COOL AND SHADY AND PRIVATE IN SERAPHINA'S CIRCLE. I sit on soft brown needles, so thick they blanket the ground, and lean against Seraphina's rough trunk. I don't care if resin sticks to the back of my shirt. Mom's mad at me already. And my punishment couldn't be worse. I'm banished.

I close my eyes and listen to the summer wind sighing through the evergreen boughs above me. Seraphina always soothes me. As I breathe in her piney scent, my mind fast-forwards to the all-star track meet on August 7. At least Mom's letting me go home for that. I've got five weeks to train. And this time for sure I'll be the best at high jump.

It's important to keep in shape — not just my body, but my mind. I have to visualize winning to make it happen. That's what professional athletes do. So I picture clearing my first jump no problem. Then I see the pole raised higher and higher. I see the evil Arden Hampton-Price eliminated. I see myself still in. And now I'm ready to make my record-breaking jump. I focus, run, and take off —

"Morgan?" Mom's voice slices my concentration. "Where are you? We're ready to go."

Oh no! I crash right into the pole. As I pick myself up off the mat I can hear Arden laughing. Thanks Mom. Will I *ever* learn to let nothing distract me?

"Bye, Seraphina." I crawl out from under the tree's boughs. "See you soon."

As I run across Grandma's front yard to the car, Mom glares at me. "I certainly hope you won't embarrass me today," she says. The word *again* is understood.

I don't answer. What could I possibly do wrong at the family picnic? Except maybe spill something, or chew with my mouth open — and that's not what she means. Talking back would be more like it. But that won't be happening — I've decided not to speak to Mom for the rest of the summer.

In our station wagon I have to sit sandwiched between my little brother Glen and Grandma Duncan. Glen's a pain, but Grandma's great. We're on our way to the annual Duncan–Laing family picnic. When I was little, I'd look forward to it the whole last week of school. But now that I'm almost thirteen, everything is different. Now I dread spending the whole day with my country cousins at a boring park in a stupid farm town way beyond nowhere.

And to make it even worse, this year I'm stuck out here the whole summer. My parents and Glen are going home tomorrow and leaving me at Grandma's farm. Just thinking about it makes my throat ache like it did the time I accidentally swallowed an ice cube and it got stuck halfway down. I mean, I love Grandma and all, but I don't want to stay here.

I want to be back in Northington, with Jade. She's my new best friend. Not that I'm *her* best friend — Jade's way too popular for that — but she's mine. See, my former best friend, Maheesa, and all the other girls I used to hang with, dumped me a couple of months ago. For Arden Hampton-Price. Luckily I met Jade at rep softball tryouts. And now she's my only friend.

Anyway, Mom wants an apology.

Mom *expects* an apology.

Mom can dream on.

She'll never hear me say sorry until she lets me come home.

I make a face at Glen, who is taking up more than his share of space. He smirks back at me. He's going to camp for the summer. He's happy. I'd like to smack him.

But I don't. It's not worth the trouble that would land me in. Instead I snuggle up to Grandma and she folds me into a hug. I'd love to ask her how much Mom told her about what happened. Probably everything. But if I talk at all I'll start bawling.

Tears are already stinging my eyes and I blink hard to hold them back because, ohmigod, I am going to miss my mother so much. What I don't get is how I can pretty much hate her but still totally love her on the same heartbeat.

See, at first Mom was seriously mean. But once she'd banished me to Grandma's for the summer, she started acting nice again. Before we left for Grandma's she helped me pack, even though it was in complete silence. She arranged an extended loan on a whole pile of library books, and got me boxes of power bars and sports drinks, which she usually refuses to buy. She even tucked in some paper and stamped envelopes so I can write to Jade, since Grandma doesn't have email.

So how am I going to get through the whole summer without Mom?

And how am I supposed to survive without Jade? I'm not allowed to phone her, even though Grandma has a long-distance plan. According to Mom, Jade is a bad influence. I can send her letters, but that's all. Well, Mom doesn't have to worry, because Jade's impossible to reach. Her cell rings non-stop. She only answers if it's a guy she likes, so then she gets tons of messages. She almost never returns calls. Why should she? Everybody always phones her again.

Mostly I talked to Jade at softball practice. We both made the rep team — she pitches and I catch. But now Mom's ended that too. Right. Like she can stop me having even one friend by sending me out here to the farm. Sure, there are my cousins, but they're not cool like Jade.

As if Grandma knows what I'm thinking, she squeezes my shoulder and kisses my cheek. Then she opens her purse and offers me a mint. Green-and-white striped — my favourite kind. I unwrap the candy and pop it into my mouth. It helps keep the tears back. Of course Glen takes two.

When we finally reach Cheltingdon Fairgrounds, Glen heads straight for the river, where a bunch of kids are fishing. I carry a container full of Grandma's butter tarts to the picnic area. All the tables are pushed together in long rows and covered with white paper tablecloths. Aunt Faye is organizing food: platters of cold chicken and ham, bowls of potato and pasta salad, baskets of rolls, slices of watermelon, tons of cakes and pies.

My oldest cousin, Clare, is helping. She's wearing a flowery sundress that swirls almost to her ankles, and strappy sandals. Her long dark hair is swept back with a silver clip that matches her simple hoop earrings. She smiles and waves when she sees me.

"Hey, Morgan!" Clare's smile makes me feel like I'm the guest of honour. "How's it going?"

I look down at my jean shorts, my plain white T-shirt, my

grubby old runners. Even when I'm fifteen like Clare, and even if I dress like she does, I will never be what the grownups call *lovely*. Grandma will never stare at me and say, *Oh my, you remind me so much of my beautiful sister Seraphina*.

"I'm okay," I tell her.

"Really?" Clare bundles plastic knives and forks into neat packages wrapped with paper napkins. "Being forced to spend the whole summer at Grandma's is just what you've always wanted?"

So everybody knows. Great. "Well I used to want to," I say, "like when I was about eight. Back when we used to play in Seraphina's Circle all the time."

Clare nods. "Actually, I was just thinking about Seraphina the other day." A soft, sweet smile spreads across Clare's face. "I'm glad you're here," she says. "It's going to be a great summer."

A sudden panicky feeling shakes me, and I want to scream, *No! No it's not! It's going to be horrible, the worst summer in the world*. Where did *that* come from?

"Uh-huh," I say. "Whatever." According to Mom, I'm supposed to spend the summer improving my attitude and acting more mature. Trying to be more like Clare. Like that's ever going to happen. "Love your dress," I say as I try to smooth my frizzball hair. "Did you make it?"

"Thanks!" Clare twirls so her skirt lifts and flutters about her legs. "It wasn't hard to do, it's such an easy pattern."

"For you, maybe. But hey, I'm going to be in an all-star track meet in August. I qualified for relay and high jump."

"Morgan, that's terrific!"

"Yeah, it's for all of York region, they only picked a few kids from each school." My insides tighten. I absolutely can't wait for the all-star meet. "I wish I was better though, I mean, I'm not really all that good, I just try hard. And now there's this new kid at our school, Arden Hampton-Price, she's in it too, and she's way better than me. She'll probably win. But I'm going to practise all summer, I brought my stuff with me." As I babble on, my legs go all quivery and need to be moving. "Hey Clare, let's go for a walk," I say.

Clare glances around as if she's expecting someone. "I better not. I really should keep helping out here."

There's no use trying to change Clare's mind. She won't come if there's work to be done. Maybe I should stay and help her?

But no. That would please Mom far too much.

What would please me is if I could learn to drive Uncle Paul's old tractor. Clare learned three summers ago, when he needed help at harvest time. Of course Mom and Aunt Faye said it wasn't safe. They said Clare could get hurt. They said Uncle Paul should have junked that old tractor when he bought his new one.

Maybe I'll go ask him right now. "Clare, is your Dad here?"

"Not yet, he had some chores to finish up. He'll be around for the food though. Why?"

"Do you think he'd teach me to drive his tractor?"

"What for?"

"Because it'd be so — " I have to stop myself from saying, *so cool*. Clare drives the tractor to do real farm work. But all I want is the thrill — which means I was only thinking of myself, just the kind of behaviour Mom wants me to change. "Never mind," I say. "Where's Dulcy?"

"Down by the river." Clare sets out salt and pepper beside

a stack of paper plates. "You go see her. I can manage this."

"Okay." My cousin Dulcy, Clare's little sister, is only ten, and I don't want to get stuck with her. But anything is better than standing around not being Clare. "Later." I dash off like I'm already running the relay. At the river I find my three little boy cousins, Ben and Brody and Blake, climbing on the willow branches that overhang the water. Dulcy is standing with Glen, watching the kids fishing.

"Morgan!" Dulcy squeals. "Hi, Morgan!"

"Morgan!" Glen says. "Get lost, Morgan!"

I ignore him. "Want to go for a walk, Dulcy?"

Dulcy looks at Glen as if he's a rock star instead of my loser of a little brother. He shrugs. "Okay," Dulcy says.

As we wander along the riverbank, Dulcy tells me all about her plans for us this summer. Apparently we're going to spend every waking minute together, and then have sleepovers most nights. Yeah, right. Time to change the subject. "Hey Dulcy?" I say. "Doesn't your sister ever do anything just for fun?"

"What do you mean?" Dulcy picks up a stick and swipes at the weeds beside the path.

"Oh, you know, Clare's always helping, and she's so nice and everything. Isn't she ever bad? Doesn't she ever get into trouble?"

Dulcy snickers. "Look over there." She points with her stick towards the picnic area. "*He's* trouble!"

My mouth drops open. What's this? Clare is walking with a guy. Some guy I don't recognize, so he can't be a relative. I know he isn't a Duncan or a Laing because I've never seen him at the family picnic before. And believe me, I'd remember!

He's built like a hockey player, and he walks like he owns the world. He looks more like a man than a boy. And woo-hoo! He's holding her hand!

I force my mouth shut, but it falls open again. "*Who is that?*"

"Renzo Cordona," Dulcy says.

"How'd she hook up with him?"

"She met him at Nicole's birthday party." Dulcy tosses her stick into the water. "He goes to college, but in the summer he works in town at his family's store — you know, Cordona's Hardware?"

I can't help staring. Last year, Clare brought her best friend Nicole to the picnic. This year she's brought a boyfriend. An older, gorgeous stud of a guy.

"C'mon." Dulcy grabs my hand and pulls me toward the tables. "It's time to eat."

I'm hungry, but what to do? I was hoping to sit with Clare. But Clare is busy.

"Here! Over here, girls!" Dad hollers, so loud that people back home in Northington can probably hear him. "I've got all the devilled eggs at this table!" How goofy he looks in his baggy shorts with all those pockets and white sports socks with sandals. And I just know he's going to do something embarrassing next. Like get down on his hands and knees, stick his head through people's legs to look under the tables, and call out: *Anybody seen two cute little curly-haired girls? They've just stolen five dozen butter tarts!*

"We better sit with him," I tell Dulcy.

Mom is sitting across the table with Aunt Faye. It's easy to see they're sisters. They look so much alike — dark hair streaked with silver, blue eyes flecked with grey. And they act alike too. Both are completely old-fashioned, overprotective and way too strict.

Aunt Faye only lets Clare drive the tractor because there isn't anybody else to do the work. So what I can't figure out is how Clare got away with bringing a guy to the picnic. And not some geeky just-friends guy, but a hot, hand-holding guy.

Aunt Faye is eyeing Clare and Renzo right now. Then she points them out to Mom. The sisters shake their heads and frown.

I help myself to one of Aunt Faye's homemade rolls, break and butter it. Dulcy pokes me. "You didn't answer yet."

"What?" I bite into the roll. Hey, maybe being old-fashioned isn't all bad, if you make bread like Aunt Faye. But Mom never bakes anything, so what's *her* excuse for acting like she lives in the nineteenth century?

"I said," Dulcy cups her hand around my ear and whispers, "do you want to play Seraphina tomorrow?"

2

AFTER THE FAMILY PICNIC, MY PARENTS AND GLEN HEAD home to Northington. So, as soon as Grandma's gone to bed, I decide to phone Jade. I already gave her this number, so she'd know it was me calling. But of course all I get is: *Hi, you've reached the fabulous Jade Dalton. But I'm having way too much fun to take your call, so please leave a message.* I know not to bother. Maybe some other time she'll answer.

Jade couldn't believe that Mom would make me come to the farm for the summer. She didn't get it that my parents care so much what I do. And she didn't understand why I couldn't just go live at her house. The Daltons have lots of space — they live in one of those new monster homes out in Paisley Hill Place. Jade has a huge bedroom with walkout patio doors and an ensuite bathroom.

Mom likes old houses best. And I'd never admit it to her, but so do I. When I wake up the next morning, I'm happy to be at Grandma's because I love my bedroom here so much. It has a golden pine floor, slanted ceiling and pretty flowered wallpaper. So the first things I see are daisies and rosebuds, and the first thing I hear is the gentle cooing of mourning doves. Today a breeze smelling of sunshine and clover and dew tickles the ruffled white curtains.

Okay, so even though I'm mad at Mom, it's comforting

that this was her room when she was a girl. And I sure wish she hadn't gone home without me.

Standing and stretching, I cross to the arched window. The sill is so low I have to kneel to look out. I don't know, maybe Mom's right. Maybe spending the summer at the farm will be good for me. I mean, I'm not sure I'd like Jade as much as I do if I hadn't lost Maheesa and felt so desperate. Jade's a great pitcher, and I really admire her for that. But she's not as nice as Maheesa. Or not as nice as Maheesa used to be, before Arden came along.

But what if that's exactly how Mom wants me to feel? All warm and fuzzy and attached, so I'll never grow up. So I'll stay away from kids like Jade. Kids who have amazing parties and great clothes and tons of friends and don't care what their teachers or parents say. Kids who, as Mom says, would rather have a good time than good grades. Kids who'd do anything to be *in*.

The bright morning light makes me squint. Seraphina stands like royalty on the east side of Grandma's front lawn. Her lower branches sweep the ground like a queen's skirt. Higher up, clusters of cones hang in her boughs like jewels.

Years ago Grandma told me and Clare and Dulcy how her sister planted a seedling in memory of their mother who had died when they were girls. That's when we started calling the grown balsam fir tree Seraphina, after our great-aunt. The name sounded like the song of her branches waving in the wind. And our fort, hidden up under her spreading boughs, we named Seraphina's Circle. We used to spend hours there, acting out her story.

Poor Seraphina. When she planted that tree she was only twelve years old. Just like me. How sad she must have been.

And then to die so young herself — it's too depressing to think about.

Far across the fields is the Laing farm, where my cousins live. I can't believe Dulcy asked me to play Seraphina today. What a baby. Clare and I outgrew that game years ago.

Grandma is sipping tea and talking on the phone when I go downstairs. "I'm so sorry you couldn't make the picnic, Fergus," she's saying. "We did have a grand old time."

I grab a double chocolate chip cookie from the open tin on the table. Mom would never let me have cookies for breakfast at home, but here I can. That's another thing I like about being at the farm.

Life's too short to wait for someday, is Grandma's motto. After Grandpa died, she decided to do whatever she wanted. Like dye her grey hair blonde. Like buy an RV and drive to Florida every winter. Like eat cookies for breakfast while she chats on the phone with her boyfriend, a widower from two farms over.

"I'll talk to you later, Fergus." Grandma pours me some tea from her best pot, now in everyday use. Shaped like Aladdin's lamp, it's swirled with gold, and far too fancy to save for Sunday, she says. She sets a bowl of fresh strawberries in front of me, along with a blue glass pitcher of maple syrup.

Grandma laughs as I pour syrup over my berries. "My, my," she says, "all that sugar. Wouldn't your mother be cross?"

I laugh too. Maybe it really will be okay to be here. Away from my bossy old mother who doesn't believe in fun. Away from Arden Hampton-Price, who can beat me at high jump. Who has made my life suck for the past three months. And who took away all my friends so I've only got Jade.

But then, I've never stayed at Grandma's for more than

two weeks. How will I ever fill a whole summer? There isn't any farm work for me to do. The fields are all rented out, and except for a few hens and some barn cats, Grandma doesn't keep any livestock. Sure, I can feed the cats and gather eggs. But there's nothing important and necessary, nothing like the chores Clare and Dulcy do.

"Gram?" I ask. "Do you think Clare will be too busy for me to go over there today?"

"Why don't you call her?" Grandma looks away as I wipe at the strawberry I dropped on my quilted placemat. The juice leaves a blood-like blotch, the kind of thing Mom would have a hissy-fit about.

Unlike Jade, Clare answers the phone right away. But then, she doesn't have call display. "Oh Morgan, I'm so sorry, I can't talk now," she says. "I'm expecting a call. Then Mom and I are going berry picking. But Dulcy's on her way over to see you."

"Great." I really try to sound excited. There's no way I want to hurt Grandma's feelings by acting unhappy to be here. "I'll go meet her."

Dulcy comes skipping down the road singing a Raffi song. She's wearing some kind of shorts suit, purple-and-lime-green striped, with a big zipper up the front. And in her hair, purple plastic barrettes shaped like little ducks.

She stoops to pick some daisies and asks, "Want to play in Seraphina's Circle?"

"No."

"But we always do."

"*Did*, you mean." I pitch a stone from the roadside into Grandma's cornfield. Not as good a throw as Jade would have made, but decent enough. "You mean we used to," I say, not looking at Dulcy's eager face, "when we were little."

Dulcy fiddles with her daisies, making them into a bouquet. "Well, let's go to the barn then and look for kittens."

"Nah." The barn is ancient and dark, always full of flies and dust and the smell of cattle. My cousins think I'm a city wimp, but I don't care. I'm not going in there — not even to find the cutest kittens on earth. "It makes me sneeze," I say. "I'm allergic to it."

Dulcy hands me her bouquet. "What do you want to do, then?"

I start pulling petals from one of the daisies, thinking: *He loves me / He loves me not.* And then: *If you were Clare, I'd tell you all about Jeff Tan, how cute he is and how he smiled at me in science class. And you'd tell me all about Renzo.* I pluck the last petal and fling the stem to the ground. "Practise high jump," I say.

Dulcy does a happy little kick in the air. "Okay!"

"There's this kid I have to beat at the all-star meet," I say as we drag my high-jump standards from the garage onto the front lawn. "Arden Hampton-Price. She beat me at the area schools meet and then again at the regional meet." *And if you were Clare, I might tell you all the other rotten stuff she did to me.* "But in August, I'm going to win."

"It's good your Mom made this high-jump stuff for you," Dulcy says, copying my hamstring stretch, "so you can practise every day."

"Yeah, I guess." Back in April, Mom and I went to the lumber store for the wood and a pole. That was when we were still getting along. Before Arden. Before Jade. "You know how my Mom likes to build stuff." In the past five years Mom has renovated our entire house, doing most of the work herself.

Except for my room, which she keeps promising to fix up one of these days.

"But my Dad helped too," I tell Dulcy. "He rescued that old mattress from somebody's garbage so I'd have a landing mat." I dance on the spot, shaking out my arms and legs. "Plus he bought me the best jumping shoes, Mom really freaked over how much they cost. She only lets me wear them to practise or for meets. You keep stretching, I'll go get them."

My new runners weigh next to nothing. Wearing them is like walking barefoot. But they're tough too. Running back outside I practically fly. Until I remember what happened on our way to the farm last Saturday.

We were finally ready to go, with my suitcase and stuff in the back and my homemade high-jump gear strapped to the roof racks. But on our way out of Northington we had to drive by Jeff Tan's house. And he just happened to be dribbling a basketball down the sidewalk. And strolling right beside him just happened to be Arden Hampton-Price.

Arden was wearing this skimpy black tank top and shorts that showed off her long, shapely legs. The legs that beat me at high jump. Her blonde hair shimmered in the sun, and the way she was looking at Jeff Tan made me want to spew. But I kept gawking out the window anyway like a big geek. How pathetic is that?

"Can you do the flop?" Dulcy asks. "I can only do scissors."

"Sort of, but not like Arden does." Even with my awesome new shoes, I'm going to have to work harder than ever in my life to out-jump that girl. "I mean, she just backflips through the air so she's almost upside down. And then she does this wicked somersault off the mat." I set the pole low so we can warm up. "Everybody says I jump funny, because I'm the only one at my school who jumps from the left. But who cares?"

We jump until Dulcy can't go any higher, and then I raise the pole to 1 metre. I make that and 1.1 right away, then 1.2 and 1.25 on my second tries.

And then, the way it always happens when I'm jumping, my worries slip away. I forget everything. Even Arden. Jumping is all that matters. I feel strong, but light as dandelion fluff. At 1.3 I really have to try, and at 1.35, my personal best, I miss seven times before I finally clear the pole.

But I make it. *Yes!*

"You're right, you sure do jump funny," Dulcy says as we put everything away. "You look like you're doing half scissors and half flop. But you're so good. You'll beat that Arden, no problem."

"Thanks." Now what? It's only eleven o'clock in the morning on the first Monday of the whole long summer. "We should go for a run to train some more," I say. "But it's way too hot and muggy."

"I bet it's cool in Seraphina's Circle." Dulcy looks hopeful. "So what do you want to do?"

"You know what?" I can't help saying. "What I want to do is go home. Then I want to go to the mall with Jade and eat fries, and then I want to go to Parker Pool and maybe see Jeff Tan there, and then I want to go to a movie."

Dulcy picks a wild buttercup, runs her fingers over it. "I guess it's pretty boring here, compared to Northington." She sounds like she might start to cry.

"Sorry." It's not Dulcy's fault I'm stuck here. It's my own. Mom made that perfectly clear. I'm supposed to try to be a nicer person, so I give it a go. "Okay, here's what we can do.

Let's make some cornhusk dolls."

Dulcy wrinkles up her forehead. "How?"

"I'll show you. We had to learn a pioneer craft at school last year — first we have to collect husks."

The cornfield lies just beyond the farmhouse. We bring Grandma's egg basket from the henhouse and wander along the dusty rows. The corn stands not quite shoulder high. It isn't mature yet, but it's an early variety, so we find some small cobs to pick. They snap off easily. We shuck the outer husks and let them fall to the ground. Then we place the pale green inner husks in the basket.

Dulcy pretends to eat the tiny kernels from one of the immature cobs. "Yum, yum," she says. "I love corn on the cob."

"Yeah, me too." I swing the basket on my arm. "Hey, that makes me hungry. I wonder what Grandma has for lunch?"

"Leftovers from the picnic, I bet," Dulcy says. "I hope there's some of that macaroni salad." Then she drops her cob and scrapes at the ground. "Oh look! Look Morgan!" She picks something up and brushes off the sandy soil. "I think it's that half of Seraphina's buckle I lost."

I stare at the piece of brass in Dulcy's palm. "Ohmigod!" I say. "It is." The half-buckle is tarnished a dark blue-green, almost black in places. It's cut in a fancy pattern and shaped like a wing. When it's clasped properly with the other half, the two form a whole butterfly.

Clare keeps the other half in her jewellery box. But we thought this one was lost forever. And now it's found.

I want it.

I've always wanted it. Ever since Grandma gave it to Clare.

That was the day three years ago when Grandma told us how Seraphina died. We thought we knew all about our great-aunt, but the stories we'd heard were just the beginning. I don't even want to think about it now — Seraphina's death was just so sad. But I can't help remembering as I stand there staring at that piece of buckle.

"Seraphina was wearing this the night she died," Grandma had said, taking the buckle from an old trunk. Her eyes had filled with tears.

"Oh! It's so beautiful," I said. "Can I have it?"

"No, no, give it to me. Please, Gram?" Dulcy begged.

Clare reached out to touch the buckle with a soft, longing sigh.

"Well," Grandma said. "Well, really it should go to Clare. She's the oldest. And her middle name is Seraphina." She dabbed at her eyes with a tissue. "And she looks just like my beautiful sister did."

Clare took the buckle, and we ran outside to Seraphina's Circle. "Morgan, you be Great-grandfather Hamish, and Dulcy, you be Grandma," Clare said. "I'll be Seraphina." It was always the same. Clare was *always* Seraphina.

"Now remember," Clare hooked the buckle to the waist-band of her shorts, "this is the last time you'll ever see me."

After that first time we added Seraphina's death to our game, Clare said, "I know what. Let's share the buckle." I can still see the loving way she smiled as she handed half to me. I remember thinking that if *I* had that buckle, I wouldn't be so kind. I'd want to keep it all for myself. But Clare simply said, "I'll keep one half, and you two keep the other."

So I carried half the buckle in my pocket all afternoon, like a piece of magic. I felt like I was actually connected to

Seraphina. Like I was linked to her just the way the two halves of the buckle were when they were joined. Not in a scary way though. In a good way, like she was still alive somewhere out in the universe.

But then I gave Dulcy a turn. I didn't want to, but I kind of had to, since Clare kept dropping hints that it was time. And when we went out to pick corn for supper, Dulcy must have dropped our half of the buckle. We searched and searched, but we never could find it.

Of course we didn't tell Grandma. "I'm going to lock my half away in my jewellery box," Clare said. "For safe-keeping." I guess she did, because I've never seen it since. And soon after that we stopped playing Seraphina, so I'd forgotten all about it.

Until now. My hand reaches out. "Let me hold it?"

"No!" Dulcy closes her fingers.

"We were supposed to share it."

"I don't care. I'm never letting go until I give it to Clare to put in her jewellery box with the other half."

"I won't keep it," I say. "Just let me see."

"Isn't it pretty?" Dulcy displays the buckle half on her palm again. "I bet Clare can make a dress with a belt that she can wear it on."

And then, without knowing I'm going to, I snatch it.

"Hey!" Dulcy yells.

But I can't stop myself. Something about that bit of buckle makes me feel desperate. Why should Clare have it? "You know," I say, "we really can't share this, because half should belong to my family. After all, my mother is Seraphina's oldest niece."

Dulcy picks up her cornhusks. "That's not fair, Morgan!"

Her plump cheeks flush with heat and anger. "I found it, and I want to give it to Clare."

But the longer I hold it, the less I want to give it back. "Clare doesn't need to know," I say. "We don't have to tell her."

I turn and run away from Dulcy. She follows, yelling at me to come back. But she can't move very fast because she's lugging the basket of husks. When I'm at the end of the row, I stop to have a better look at the piece of brass. The wing shape is almost as wide as my hand. Grandma told us the cut-out pattern is called filigree. At one edge is the slot where the other half would fit, and on the back is a raised strip where a belt could be attached.

A little voice inside me, a voice which sounds just like Mom, urges: *Give it back.* Well, if I were Clare, like Mom wants me to be, maybe I would.

No, that isn't right. If I were Clare, I never would have taken it in the first place. Clare would never be so nasty.

But then Clare already has half of Seraphina's buckle.

I tuck the little piece of brass into my pocket as Dulcy catches up with me. There's sweat on her forehead and tears in her eyes. She whacks me in the leg with the basket and says, "That was so mean!"

"I know, I know," I say. "I'm sorry. But if you give me this, and if you don't tell Clare, I'll bring you to Northington with me for the all-star track meet. You'll get to see me beat Arden Hampton-Price in high jump."

Dulcy frowns and scratches at a mosquito bite on her leg. "Oh, all right," she finally says. "But you have to play with me in Seraphina's Circle."

"Okay," I say. "Deal. But not till after lunch."

3

"Lucky for you, Dulcy," I say as Grandma sets out leftovers from the family picnic for lunch. "There's lots of macaroni salad. And lucky for me there's still some butter tarts. Weren't they all gone yesterday, Gram?"

"I kept some here for you girls," Grandma says. "Well, and for Fergus too. So save a couple for him, okay?"

We're not even finished eating when Dulcy reminds me of my promise to play in Seraphina's Circle. And I'm still working on a slice of watermelon when she drags me outside. I spit some seeds at her and toss the rind into the compost pail on the back step. Dulcy picks up our basket of husks.

As we creep under Seraphina's boughs, I slip my hand into my pocket. The buckle half is safe. I decide to keep it with me all the time, so it doesn't ever get lost again.

Once we're inside Seraphina's Circle, everything feels different. Time stops and real life floats away.

"Can I be Seraphina?" Dulcy says.

I pick up a cornhusk. "Let's make the dolls instead."

"But you promised —"

"I promised to play in Seraphina's Circle. And I am. Look, start by rolling a little ball of husks for the head." I show Dulcy how, then roll more husks around sticks for arms and legs and a body.

"Hey, this is fun!" Dulcy says as we work. "I'm sorry I called you mean, Morgan. You're not. You're really nice."

I can't help smiling. This is *so* childish, but she's right, it *is* fun. "Now we tie the parts together, like this." I use some of the long grass that grows in a ring around Seraphina's Circle. Grandma always leaves a wild patch when she mows her lawn, so she won't damage Seraphina's lowest boughs.

The first few dolls fall apart. But we keep trying until we make some that look not too bad.

I twirl my best doll in my hand. "See, isn't this better than playing Seraphina?"

"No," Dulcy says. "Because I never got a chance to be Seraphina. I've been waiting years and years."

"Yeah, I know." I add a row of husks around my doll's waist to make a skirt. "Me too. But Clare was the best Seraphina — we'd never be as good as she was. And anyway, we can't play without her. Two isn't enough."

"Okay, then let's make up a new game." Dulcy shapes a little husk skirt for one of her dolls. "This will be Clare," she says. "She dresses so pretty."

I groan. "And who's the other one? Renzo Cordona?"

Dulcy giggles. "Sure. They go together. Now I can pretend *their* story, just like we used to pretend Seraphina's."

"And I can call this doll Jeff Tan," I say. Ohmigod this is infantile. But it's not like I've got anything else to do. "And who should my girl doll be? Me? Or maybe Arden?"

"Have her be Arden, so you can make her mess up at high jump." Dulcy dances her two dolls around together. "Do you think they kissed?"

"Jeff and Arden?"

"No — Clare and Renzo."

I don't answer. I concentrate on wrapping a little shawl around Arden's shoulders, then making a husk bonnet to cover up her long blonde hair. Oh, what am I doing? Good thing no one like Jade or Arden can see me.

"Hey Morgan," Dulcy says. "How come your Mom made you stay here, anyway?"

I set my dolls down on the soft brown needles that cover the ground and look up into Seraphina's cool, green branches. Where to begin? But I can feel Dulcy waiting and wanting to know. "Because she's a lot like Great-grandfather Hamish?" I finally say.

Dulcy looks confused. "I don't get it."

"Well, she thinks she can control my life, just like Hamish tried to control Seraphina's. She thinks she can choose my friends, tell me where I can go and who I can hang out with."

"You mean like how Hamish tried to keep Seraphina from seeing Jed?"

"Yeah, something like that. Except it's not over a guy — Jeff Tan barely knows I'm alive. There's this kid called Jade, she's in Grade 8, well, actually she'll be going to high school in the fall. And when I stopped being friends with Maheesa, because of Arden, I started being friends with Jade."

"And your Mom doesn't like Jade?"

"No, because Jade's parents are rich and they let her do whatever she wants. Mom says they've got more money than brains, and Jade has everything but a curfew."

Dulcy's eyes widen. "How'd you get to be friends with her, then?"

"You know that rep softball team I told you about, Preston Paints? The one I was supposed to play for this summer?"

"Uh-huh?" Dulcy dances her dolls around in a little circle. "What about it?"

"Jade's one of the pitchers, and we got to know each other, practising together." I have to stop to control my voice, which is going all shaky. "I felt so great that the coach thought I was good enough to catch for her. I mean, Jade's terrific. Every pitch goes right where she wants it to. She might *act* crazy, but she almost never *pitches* wild." I take a deep breath. "Anyway, Jade was having a grad party and Mom wouldn't let me go. She said it wasn't appropriate, that I could go to a party next year, when I graduate. But everybody else was going."

I'm not sure how much to tell. Mom might think I'm corrupting Dulcy or something — after all, she's only ten. Well, I don't care. Dulcy needs to know about kids like Arden — if she doesn't already. "See, I *had* to go to Jade's party to prove myself. Arden would have told everybody I was a big geek if I didn't go."

"I wouldn't be friends with Arden," Dulcy says. "So then what?"

"Then I just went. I waited until Mom was asleep, and I sneaked out."

Dulcy gasps. "But how'd she find out?"

"Arden." I spit out her name. "She knew I wasn't allowed to go, see, so she called my house the next morning. But she didn't even ask to speak to me. She just asked my mother if I'd had a good time at Jade's party."

"You're kidding. I bet Aunt Liz was so mad!"

"Yeah, she went nuts." I can hardly stand to talk about it. "She said it was the worst thing I'd ever done, that she could never trust me again. She said *Clare* would never do such a terrible thing."

"Wow," Dulcy says. "Oh wow."

"There's more. Arden told Mom a bunch of lies — she said I'd been drinking and doing drugs and stuff. And Mom believed her!" I'm still mad that Mom believed Arden, not me. It wasn't that kind of a party at all. I tried to tell Mom what Arden's like, that she was making it up. And that it was because of Arden, not Jade, that I went to the party. But Mom wouldn't listen. "Anyway, Mom said I could be grounded for the whole summer or I could spend it at the farm."

"*I* know you wouldn't do those things," Dulcy says.

"Thanks. You're right about that. But you know what?" I shouldn't tell Dulcy this, but remembering how Mom listened to Arden makes me do it. "I'm glad I went — it was the most amazing party. Jade's parents hired a caterer to barbeque out by their pool, and they had make-your-own sundaes and they even had a DJ. All the girls got a rose, and they gave out movie gift certificates as favours. Not that I've had a chance to use mine yet."

"Oh man!" Dulcy says. And then, "I'm glad you chose to come here. Are you?"

My lips make a sputtering sound. Mom was so determined to punish me she didn't even care when she couldn't get the rep softball fees refunded. "Yeah, sure, whatever."

But now that I've started thinking about what happened, I can't stop. While Dulcy plays with her dolls, imagining scenes for Clare and Renzo that sound a lot like scenes from Seraphina's life, I think about how happy I was before Arden came to my school.

Maheesa was my best friend since kindergarten. I liked her from the first day because she had the prettiest hair I'd ever seen — long and dark and curly — and we both had Winnie-the-Pooh backpacks. Then as we got older, we both liked to play sports, not Barbies. But besides Maheesa, last year I had a whole group of girls I was friends with. Jeff Tan had actually spoken to me a few times. And I still had a chance to be the best at high jump.

Then Arden showed up and ruined everything.

And even worse, I embarrassed myself trying to be friends. On her first day, I invited Arden over after school. Which was a complete disaster. When she found out that a parent is almost always home at my house, that I'm not allowed to watch TV after school, and that I didn't have anything in my closet she'd ever want to borrow, she didn't want to be part of my group.

No wait. She didn't want *me* to be part of it. She wanted to take over. She wanted to bully me out.

Most of my so-called friends went with Arden right away. After all, she was new and exciting, and all the guys were following her around like imprinted ducklings. But Maheesa, my very best friend, stayed loyal.

Maheesa stuck up for me when Arden said I didn't belong because I don't have pierced ears. Maheesa invited me to her sleepover birthday party, even though Arden banned me. Maheesa even pretended not to mind when Arden convinced everybody else not to come to her party because I'd be there.

But one morning at recess, even Maheesa changed.

Arden likes to harass little kids, and she started calling Glen things like "lardo" and "fat-ass." She made sure everybody joined in. When I heard Maheesa teasing him too, I shouted, "Hey! Leave my brother alone!"

"Chill, Morgan," Maheesa said. "It's only for fun, okay? We're just fooling around. Glen can take it."

Yeah, I knew that. I mean, I sometimes give Glen a hard time myself, but he's free to tease me right back. Arden and the rest of them had no right. "You guys are disgusting," I yelled. "I hate you all!"

Maheesa hasn't spoken to me since.

Now I've only got Jade. But she's hours away. And she has tons of other friends, so she's probably forgotten all about me already.

"*I'm sorry, Renzo,*" Dulcy makes her Clare doll say. "*My parents won't let me see you again. They think you're too old for me.*"

"*Then we'll meet in secret,*" her Renzo doll says. "*Meet me at midnight, behind the barn.*"

"*But what if we get caught?*"

"*Then we'll run away together. We'll get married and live happily ever after.*"

"Dulcy! That's so cheesy. Nobody lives happily ever after."

Dulcy frowns. "Oh," she says. "Okay then, I'll have to think up a *terrible tragedy*, like Seraphina's. Maybe they'll have to die for love. That's more fun anyway."

A strange hot hint of fear flickers around me, just like the day of the family picnic. "Let's go inside now," I say. "Maybe Grandma has some nice cold lemonade." I tuck my dolls up into Seraphina's boughs, as far apart as I can. I don't want to leave Jeff close to Arden even if it is just pretend. "Jeff and Arden have to go home. It's past their curfew."

Dulcy snorts with laughter. "So do Clare and Renzo, but they're going to kiss goodbye first."

I can't watch as Dulcy presses her dolls' heads together, making them embrace with a slurpy kissing sound.

"Let's play this again tomorrow," Dulcy says. "Let's play it every day you're here."

"Maybe," I say as I step from the cool shelter of Seraphina's Circle back into the bright sunshine. In a strange way, a way I don't get at all, I kind of want to play with the cornhusk dolls again too. "We'll see."

4

THE NEXT MORNING GRANDMA GOES TO TOWN TO GET HER hair done, so I try calling Jade again. No luck. Well, she's probably still asleep. But this time I do leave a message: *Hey Jade, it's me, Morgan, calling from the farm. Just wanted to say hi, and I wish I was home in Northington but your party was worth it. I mean, worth getting sent out here. Tell your parents thanks, okay? Your Mom is such a cool dancer. So when's the next Preston Paints game? How's the team doing? Call me, call me, call me, okay? Please? I feel like I'm fading away out here. Oh, and if you see Jeff Tan around, I want to know everything! Bye for now, and don't forget to call me!*

Clare phones right after I hang up. "Hey Morgan, want to come over and help us make jam?"

Jam. How thrilling. "Yeah, I guess. But, well, um …"

"You're not still scared of the cattle, are you?"

"No! Of course not!" To get to the Laing farm, I have to walk down Grandma's road to the end of Uncle Paul's back lane, climb the fence, follow the lane between two pastures, cross the barnyard and climb the gate. Easy. It only takes ten minutes. Except when the cows are out.

"Want me to come meet you?"

"Yes, please." To my cousins the cattle are as safe and everyday as milk. To me, they're monsters.

But when I reach the lane between the cattle pastures, it's Dulcy, not Clare, who meets me. Today her hair is tied in bunches with plaid ribbon. "Clare decided she'd better weed the vegetable garden before it gets too hot out," she says.

"She's weeding your whole big old garden?"

"Well, Mom's back was bothering her after picking berries yesterday." To Dulcy it's no big deal. If there's work to be done, you do it.

The cattle lift their heads from grazing, checking us out with their huge brown eyes. When I was little I used to think they were taking my picture each time they blinked. Now I know they're getting ready to attack.

A few cows come over to the edge of the lane and follow us along. Their ruddy brown hides are splotched with dirty white patches, and they smell bad, like cow-pies. Their teeth make a horrible sound as they chomp on the grass. They chew and chew, blowing out great blasts of breath between bites. Then they lick with their fleshy purplish tongues at the weedy bits sticking out the corners of their slobbery mouths. Meanwhile their tails flick like windshield wipers, but the flies just buzz around and land again.

Suddenly one cow lifts its head and lets out a loud, bellowing moo. I grab Dulcy's hand and cling to her as we walk. When we finally reach the last gate, I realize that Dulcy has been chattering all the way, but I haven't heard a thing.

Aunt Faye's kitchen smells of fresh strawberries. "Would you rather hull berries or wash them?" she asks me. That's how it is at the Laing farm. You get right down to work.

Neither! I feel like shouting. *I want to sit down with a cold drink and recover from the cow crossing. Read a book, practise high jump, phone Jade and see what's going on.*

"Um, hull berries, I guess."

Aunt Faye plunks a full flat of berries down on the counter. But I don't quite get how to use the huller. I keep cutting off too much berry, or the ripe berries squish in my fingers.

Dulcy, though, is rinsing berries as if it's the easiest thing in the world. Well, she's used to this. I'm not. Mom is strict about curfews and homework and TV, but she doesn't make me or Glen do much around the house. She says she worked too hard as a kid, and she doesn't want us to have to.

Aunt Faye must have worked just as hard as a kid. But she married a farmer and kept right on. I'd like to ask her about that, but I'm pretty sure now's not the time. Aunt Faye looks hot and tired, and irritated that I'm so slow.

Soon Clare comes in from the garden to help. She washes her hands, drinks a glass of water, then pitches right in. She hulls twice as fast as me, nipping out the tough green stems with a mere flick of her wrist.

I keep muddling along, eating almost as many berries as I hull. Nobody speaks. I glance at Dulcy to see what's wrong. Dulcy shakes her head and rolls her eyes in Aunt Faye's direction.

By noon the air in the kitchen is thick with the sweet fruity steam from the boiling jam and the tension between Clare and Aunt Faye. For lunch Clare makes tuna sandwiches and lemonade. Then we all sit out on the front verandah, where it's cooler, to eat.

Uncle Paul appears from the barn. With him are Clare and Dulcy's little brothers, Ben and Brody and Blake. Everybody just calls them the Bees, because they're always buzzing about, honey-sweet but annoying. Little boys are cute, but when they get to Glen's age they're gross. "Well now, Morgan," Uncle

Paul says. "Keeping out of trouble?" He stands lopsided, with his weight mostly on one leg, his hands on his hips, grinning at me.

"Of course." Should I ask him about learning to drive the tractor? No, better wait. He'll be way more likely to say yes after lunch.

As soon as Uncle Paul finishes eating, the Bees swarm him with tickling. He howls and escapes across the lawn. The Bees, Dulcy and me all chase after him, but he grabs a branch of a huge old maple and hauls himself up to safety.

For a few minutes Uncle Paul pretends to sleep up there, while we all stand guard on the ground. Then he says, "All right, I gotta get back to work now. Lemme go."

The Laing kids back right off. They never push things too far, like I might. They do what they're told, when they're told. Right, that's another thing Mom wants me to work on this summer.

"I promise never to tickle you again, Uncle Paul," I say as he climbs down, "if you teach me to drive your tractor."

Uncle Paul pulls a bandanna from his jeans pocket, lifts his baseball cap and wipes at his sweaty forehead. "You? Drive my tractor?" He's going bald, and his scalp shines white against his deeply lined and suntanned face.

"Not your new one. I mean the one Clare drives."

"Well now, we'll have to see about that. It's not just for fun, you know. Clare drives so she can help me."

"Oh, I know that!"

"And that old tractor ain't running so good. She's hard to handle. Gears get jammed."

"But Clare can do it. I'm sure I could too."

Uncle Paul plunks his hat back on. "Huh," he says as he

heads back to the barn.

At five o'clock, forty jars of jam stand cooling on the counter and as many bags of berries fill the freezer. I stay for supper, but Uncle Paul doesn't mention the tractor. And while Dulcy and the Bees chatter nonstop, Clare and Aunt Faye are still tense and quiet. What's going on? I can pretty much guess, but I'd love to know for sure.

It makes me think of Mom. What's happening back home in Northington? Preston Paints probably has a game tonight, and Jade will be pitching. Maybe Jeff Tan will come to watch. I've often seen him up in the bleachers. But will he wonder where I am? Or will Arden Hampton-Price be with him?

Oh, it's not fair. How can my mother make me miss the whole summer? And how can I be wishing she were here anyway? Like right now.

*

Later, after she gets the Bees to bed, Clare walks me back to Grandma's. Dusk hangs in a smoky haze over the fields, around the clumps of Queen Anne's lace and bright blue chicory that border the roadside. Crickets chirp like crazy.

"Okay," Clare says. "What's wrong?"

"Nothing." I study the jar of jam Aunt Faye sent for Grandma. Clare wrote out the labels in her perfect calligraphy, and I stuck them on. "Oh man, look how crooked this one is. I did a crappy job."

"No you didn't." Clare turns the jam jar in my hand so the label doesn't show. "Don't worry. I'll go all the way past the cattle with you."

"It's not that." I make a moaning sound sort of like a sick cow. "I guess I'm just a bit homesick."

"Poor you." Clare slips her arm around me.

"Yeah. I mean I really like it here and all, but I just wish I could go home, you know?"

"I know." Clare hugs me harder. "Remember when I stayed at your place last Christmas? I felt like that the whole time."

"You did? You sure didn't show it." I feel so safe with Clare beside me that the cattle don't bother me at all. Is this what having an older sister would be like? Lucky Dulcy. I'm stuck with the useless Glen. I might miss home, but I sure don't miss him.

"So," I say. "What about this boyfriend of yours?"

"You mean Renzo?"

By the way Clare says his name I can tell how much she likes him. "Yeah, I mean Renzo. How long have you been going with him?"

"Only a month. He's *really* nice. But he lives in town, so I don't get to see him very often."

"That sucks." I think of Jeff Tan. I don't get to see him at all. Not that it matters, with Arden around. "But isn't Renzo kind of old?"

Clare laughs, but with a bitterness I've never heard before. "That's what Mom thinks." Her expression turns angry. "She wants me to break up with him. She didn't want him to come to the picnic."

"So that's what was wrong today. I kind of wondered."

Clare stops walking. "I can't stand it, Morgan." She holds both sides of her head as if to stop it splitting open. "She's *so* unreasonable. She's thinks we're going to have sex and I'm going to get pregnant or something."

"*And?*" I've been wondering about that too.

"And we've never been alone long enough to do more than hold hands!"

"But if you were?"

"We'd be responsible! I'm almost sixteen, and Renzo's eighteen — we're not stupid little kids."

"Okay," I say. "As long as you know what you're doing."

Clare starts walking again, and I touch her shoulder gently. "Hey, I know what you mean about your Mom. I have this new friend, well, not a boyfriend or anything, her name's Jade. And my mother just hates her."

"What's wrong with Jade?"

"Nothing," I say. "Except that her family has a lot of money, and they like to spend it. According to Mom, they're *conspicuous consumers* and they care too much about *material things*. Oh, and they let Jade do pretty much what she wants. That's why Mom made me come here, you know, to get me away from Jade."

"*No one*," Clare says, "is going to get me away from Renzo."

I punch her shoulder lightly. "You go, Clare!" As we walk on I add, "I've never heard you talk like that before."

"I've never been in love before," Clare says. "It changes you. I mean, I just don't care what Mom says. I don't mind helping out and all, but she can't tell me what to do. She can't stop me seeing Renzo. I'd rather die."

"Really?"

"Really. And if Mom doesn't like it, that's just too bad."

"You know what, Clare? My mother thinks you're perfect. She's always on me to be more like you."

"Really? Well my mother's always on *me* to be more like *you*. Did you know she wanted me to go live at your house for the summer?"

"You're kidding! Because of Renzo?"

"You got it. But of course they can't spare me, there's too much work."

"Our mothers are crazy!" I shriek into the dusk.

Clare laughs her old laugh. "They don't like Grandma seeing Fergus either, but Grandma doesn't care what they think. She does what she wants!"

At the last gate Clare stops again and says softly, "This is where Seraphina had her accident. Remember how we used to bring flowers for her?"

"We?" I say. "C'mon. It was only ever Dulcy and me, because *we* had to be Great-grandfather Hamish or Grandma or Jed."

"Well, I was dead," Clare says. "Seraphina could hardly put flowers on the spot where she died, could she?"

"I guess not. But still, we hated that you were always Seraphina. We both wanted to be her too."

"We all wanted to be Seraphina." A dreamy, faraway look crosses Clare's face. "Imagine dying for love." She gives me another hug. "I'd better get back now. See you soon."

I walk on alone through the farm-fragrant evening. Now that I'm past the cattle, there's no need to hurry. The sky glows a deep orange-red, like campfire coals, and the first star glitters. I don't wish on it though. What's the use? Even though I feel better after talking to Clare, nothing is going to change. Tomorrow I'll still be stuck here.

Well, at least I can look forward to the all-star meet on August 7. By then the summer will be half over, and I'll get to go home for a couple of days. And after that it will be only a month before I go home for good.

Before going inside Grandma's house, I slip into Seraphina's Circle. I've never come here after dark before. It's still and quiet, except for the crickets and the hoot of a barn owl. Wouldn't it be cool to sleep in here on the soft brown needles, with Seraphina watching over me?

I try to imagine living in Seraphina's time. And then I wonder what life might be like for my own great-nieces, if I ever have any. But it's hard to make my mind stretch that far. It keeps wanting to snap back to the present.

My hand feels in the pocket of my shorts, where I'm still keeping the buckle half Dulcy found in the cornfield. Which we're supposed to share. Does Seraphina know I took it? And would she care? Mom would, for sure.

Thinking about that gives me a squirmy feeling. I'm not becoming more mature here at the farm. I'm acting childish, all selfish and greedy. I know I should share Seraphina's buckle with Dulcy, like Clare said.

And what would Seraphina think of Clare and Renzo? Would she say they should be together no matter what? I remember Clare's words about Aunt Faye: *She can't stop me seeing Renzo. I'd rather die.*

I know what Mom would say about that, too. She'd be on Aunt Faye's side. No question.

5

AFTER A FEW DAYS I GIVE UP HOPING JADE MIGHT PHONE ME back. Life on the farm starts to feel almost normal. I practise high jump every day, setting my stuff up early, before the day gets hot, or after supper, when the air cools down. I can't make 1.4 yet, but I can almost always clear 1.37.

I don't see much of Clare, because she always has work to do. But Dulcy comes over a lot. Sometimes she wants to practise high jump, but mostly she wants to play with the cornhusk dolls in Seraphina's Circle.

It's funny, but I've started to like our game as much as Dulcy does. It's like I'm growing younger every day here. I'll probably be about two years old by the all-star meet.

Most mornings Grandma gives me a sewing lesson. Probably Mom's idea, but I don't even mind. With Grandma, sewing is something I want to learn.

Grandma doesn't criticize my uneven stitches. She doesn't lose patience with me. And she praises everything I make.

"Why, you'll soon be better than the Bees," Grandma says one day as I'm working on a quilt square.

"Hey, thanks." Besides teaching Clare and Dulcy to sew, Grandma actually taught the Bees some basics, like threading a needle and sewing on buttons. Everyone said she wouldn't be able to keep them still long enough, but she did.

"By the way," Grandma says as she sets out her sewing basket. "Did you know this was Seraphina's?"

"Really? Cool!" The oblong basket is made of bamboo, with a little wicker handle and a faded pink lining. "Tell me about her."

"Oh, Seraphina could sew anything. She made all our dresses, but she was also an excellent tailor — she made all our father's and our brothers' clothes, too."

"No, I mean tell me about Seraphina and Jed."

"Hmm. I thought you kids were tired of hearing those stories."

"Not! That's Mom and Aunt Faye. They're the ones who always say they're sick of Seraphina. We're crazy about her!"

Grandma looks pleased. "Where should I start?"

"I want to hear everything, right from the beginning."

Grandma gazes at Seraphina's black-and-white photo up on the wall in its carved oak frame. "Well, that picture was taken in 1943, on her eighteenth birthday. You know she was the oldest, then there was me, then the four boys." She takes her time knotting her thread, her face sad. "All but me dead and gone now." Then her expression brightens. "Oh, but Seraphina was so beautiful and smart and sweet. She helped out so much. I mean, six children in a two-room cabin plus a farm to run was desperate hard work for Mama and your Great-grandfather Hamish."

"And this house was their cabin, right?" Over the years it's been rebuilt and added on to, but I love knowing that the home where Seraphina lived has stayed in the family.

"Right. Well, when Seraphina was twelve, and I was only six, poor Mama died in childbirth. The baby was stillborn."

I snip a new length of thread. When we acted that scene

out, I liked to be poor Mama, writhing in pain and bleeding to death. Dulcy liked to be Grandma as a little girl, weeping for her dead mother and baby sister. Clare of course was Seraphina, taking charge and giving comfort. "I don't know how the Bees can thread a needle," I say in frustration. "I sure can't!"

"Here, let me help you." Grandma guides my hand. "Anyway, after that, Seraphina had to do all the work. It was like she became our mother. But she never complained, not even when she had to quit school to look after things."

"And she planted the tree," I say. "Tell about that."

"Oh yes, her balsam fir. We couldn't often get to the cemetery over in Cheltingdon to visit Mama's grave, and Seraphina wanted some kind of memorial here at home. So she went off to the woods and dug a seedling." Grandma's calm voice begins to waver. "After she planted it, she liked to keep wildflowers in jam jars by that tree. And sometimes she'd just sit out there, as if she was waiting for Mama to come back."

"And then when she was seventeen she fell in love with Jed," I say, unable to wait for the rest. "But your father Hamish was too strict. He forbade Seraphina to see him."

Grandma sets down her sewing. "Who's telling this, me or you?"

"Sorry."

"Thank you." Grandma adjusts her glasses before she continues. "Jed was the hired hand over at our neighbour, Mrs. Laing's, farm. Mrs. Laing was your Uncle Paul's great-aunt. Father didn't like Jed, because he didn't own any land. He didn't have a family and he didn't go to church. And he was a lot older than Seraphina."

Grandma stands and touches Seraphina's photo. "This was taken just before she died." She rubs at a tear rolling down her cheek. "She'd started meeting Jed in secret. I was their go-between. Father didn't notice me much, he was too busy working in the fields or the barn, so I could easily slip over there with Seraphina's messages and bring back Jed's."

I examine the photo too. Seraphina, unsmiling, wears a fancy hat with a brim so wide it looks like she has no hair. She's standing with one hip turned towards the camera and her knee slightly bent. Her shoes are plain black pumps. Her flowered dress is knee-length, with three-quarter sleeves and a waist cinched by a wide black belt. And on that belt is a buckle shaped like a butterfly.

It's the buckle Grandma gave Clare.

"That was a new dress Seraphina made to wear when she went out with Jed," Grandma says. "Of course she told father she needed a new dress for church."

My heart beats faster. The scenes where Seraphina met Jed in secret were the best to act out.

I feel for the piece of buckle in my pocket. Holding it makes me feel connected to Seraphina. I know I should share it with Dulcy, but so far she hasn't mentioned it again. So maybe Dulcy doesn't want it as much as I do.

Still, I can hear that little voice, the one that sounds like Mom, saying, *You know what the right thing to do is, Morgan. So do it. Let Dulcy have her turn.*

Yeah, okay, I will. Just not yet. Not today.

"Seraphina was so upset about her hair in that picture," Grandma says. "That's why she's wearing her Sunday hat, so you can't see how short her hair is." She fluffs my hair with her fingers. "Here's something I've never told you girls. When that photo was taken, Father had just cut off all Seraphina's lovely long hair."

"*What?*" I forget all about the buckle. "But why?"

"Because she defied him. He found out she was still seeing Jed. Mrs. Laing, who was a busybody gossip, told him. So he wanted to teach Seraphina a lesson. And since she was too big to beat, he took the scissors and chopped off her hair."

"Ohmigod! That is *so* brutal."

"Seraphina was heartbroken. She'd been growing her hair for six years, ever since our dear Mama died." Grandma digs around in the drawer of her sideboard, lifting out old lace tablecloths and candle stubs. "I saved it," she says. "Father wanted to burn her hair, but I made such a fuss he let me keep it. Look."

She hands me a faded stationery box with a border of ribbons and roses. I hold my breath as I open the lid. Inside lies a long thick twist of dark hair, just like Clare's.

"Oh Gram." I touch the hair gently. "Oh, it's gorgeous. How come you never showed us before?"

Grandma puts her arm around me. "Your mother and Aunt Faye think it's morbid. They hate knowing it's in that drawer. I think it scares them. And they never wanted me to show you girls."

"Those two control freaks! Why doesn't that surprise me?" I pat the hair again. "It feels so springy," I say. "Like it's alive."

"Seraphina used to wash it with homemade lavender shampoo and soft water from the rain barrel."

"Can we show Clare and Dulcy? Please? I know they'll want to see it."

Grandma laughs. "Of course. Just don't tell your mothers."

She tucks the box back in the drawer as if it were a newborn baby. "Oh my!" she says. "I forgot the time. Fergus will be here to pick me up for cards any minute. I better run and get ready."

"Hey!" I call after her. "Hey, Gram, you didn't finish telling me about Seraphina."

*

Dulcy's Clare doll spends her days pining for Renzo or meeting him in secret or fighting with Aunt Faye. "Clare isn't really Seraphina, you know," I tell her.

"I know," Dulcy says. "But so much about them is the same."

"Hmm." I guess I'd rather not think about that. "I'm going to rename my Arden doll."

"Why?"

"Because I don't want her having any fun with my Jeff doll. I'm going to call her Leigh, my middle name." I pitch an acorn ball to Leigh, who is up to bat for Preston Paints. Leigh hits a home run.

"And I'm going to build a house for my dolls." Dulcy uses pine cones to outline rooms on the ground by Seraphina's thick trunk. "I'm going to cut some reeds from the ditch to make mats and furniture," she says. "And for their bed I'm going to use cattail fluff."

As Dulcy works, I make Leigh high jump over sticks. "Awesome jump!" my Jeff doll cheers. "You're the best!"

"This is going to be Clare and Renzo's house when they're grown up and married," Dulcy says, decorating the rooms with wildflowers. She puts her dolls in their bed together and snickers. "Now I *know* they kiss. I saw them last night. Mom and Dad went out to a church meeting, and Renzo came over in his car."

"Really? What happened?"

"Hot stuff! I followed them into the barn and saw them kissing. Like really *really* kissing." Dulcy puckers her lips and makes a loud smooching sound. She hugs herself and wriggles.

I definitely don't want to think about that. "Leigh and Jeff are going to the mall," I say. "Leigh's going to buy some new clothes. And then Jeff's going to buy her an ice cream. A triple-scoop chocolate-fudge cone."

"Yum!" Dulcy licks her lips. "Are Leigh and Jeff getting married?"

I tuck my dolls up into Seraphina's branches. "Let's go practise high jump," I say.

"Okay! But first we have to braid." Every day we've been braiding the long soft grass that grows around the edge of Seraphina's Circle. Then, when we enter the next day, we comb it out with our fingers. The ring of rippled grass seems like a moat around a castle or something.

But now it also reminds me of Seraphina's hair. Which I haven't told Dulcy about. I'm not sure why. Maybe I want to keep it for myself a while longer, sort of like the buckle half. And I've never had a secret with Grandma before.

That evening Fergus comes to take Grandma out dancing. When I'm alone in the house I go and open the sideboard drawer. Grandma didn't say not to touch Seraphina's hair, but still, I feel a bit weird about it. Looking at the dark, twisted rope feels sort of brave and exciting, but sort of scary, too. I close the box, shut the drawer and call Clare.

"Heard what you were doing while your parents were away last night," I say.

Clare gives a nervous laugh that sounds like Dulcy giggling. "Good thing Mom's upstairs right now," she says. "I mean, she'd shoot me if she ever found out Renzo was here. But it's her own fault. She's forcing me to go behind her back."

"Exactly." Like the night I sneaked out to Jade's grad party. "So, how was it?"

"Perfect," Clare says. "Hey, want to go on a picnic tomorrow? It's time I had a day off."

"Sure. What about Dulcy?"

"You'll need to borrow her bike."

"Okay. What time?"

"Come over right after breakfast," Clare says. "I'll pack us a lunch." Then she lowers her voice to a whisper. "I want to ride to Cheltingdon to meet Renzo. *Don't tell anyone.*"

6

CHELTINGDON FAIRGROUNDS, WHERE CLARE WANTS TO have the picnic, is an hour's bike ride away, most of it over gravel roads. We set out early, while the day is still fresh. "Let's stop at Uncle Baird's cabin," Clare suggests. "It's about halfway."

"Oh yuck. Why?" Uncle Baird, who died last fall, was the youngest of Grandma's brothers. He lived like a hermit on a deserted farm in a cabin he never cleaned. "His place is scuzzy." The cabin makes me feel lost and lonely, like Grandma's barn does.

"I told Mom we'd check it out," Clare says. "She's worried about vandals. And she was kind of suspicious about today — she wanted to know what we'd be doing all day."

"Aha! Okay then."

Thick weeds choke the long, rutted laneway, but there are recent tire marks. "See?" Clare says. "A truck's been up here."

We tramp down overgrown vines and bushes to lean our bikes against the weathered cabin wall. The lock has been forced and the front door hangs open. "Sure looks like somebody broke in." I stand still, afraid to enter.

"Oh no!" Clare pushes past me. "Mom's going to be so upset."

But all we find are some empty pop cans and beer bottles

and chip bags. "At least they didn't trash the place," I say.

"Yeah, but they might. And now Mom will want to have it torn down before it gets burnt down." Clare points to the remains of a fire in the woodstove. "Too bad. It's a perfect place to meet Renzo."

I take a long drink from my water bottle. "Kind of isolated, isn't it?"

"That's the whole point — no one will know we're here. There's no chance of anybody seeing us and telling Mom."

"And so then you guys will, like, do what, exactly?"

Clare gives a nervous little giggle. "Oh, we'll just — do whatever."

"But how would you even get here?"

"I've got it all figured out." Clare smiles as she starts clearing the mess. "Nicole will pick me up to go to a movie over in Plattsworth. But really she'll bring me here."

"And Renzo will be waiting for you. Clever." I sort some stuff to recycle from the rest of the garbage. I'm certain I can smell Uncle Baird's pipe. His hands, when he lit it, used to shake like dead leaves about to fall.

Clare steps onto a ladder that leads to the loft. "We'd better go up and make sure they didn't take anything."

"Like anybody would steal that old junk." All the stuff that nobody wants but they still won't throw out ends up at Uncle Baird's. Things like a trunk of old woollen clothes packed in mothballs, a cracked china wash set, a rocking chair with only one rocker, an antique clock with no hands. All of it heaped with dust.

It's hot and stuffy up here, but Clare, in her pink-and-white striped T-shirt and pink shorts, looks cool and delicious. Like strawberry ice cream. Her hair, in a perky ponytail, pokes out the back of her sun visor. I can't help thinking how easy it would be to snip that ponytail off.

And then I'm telling Clare about Great-grandfather Hamish cutting off Seraphina's hair.

"I can't believe it!" Clare gasps. "How could he? And how come Grandma never told us before?"

"She said our mothers didn't want her to. They think it's really twisted that she saved it."

"And I think it's so cool that she did. I can't wait to see it."

I move a broken mirror to pick up a grimy oil lamp. "But you never come over."

"I know, I know, I never have time. See, I've been working extra hard, to butter Mom up about Renzo. Sorry."

"This would look great in my room if I cleaned the glass," I say, blowing dust off the lamp. "But I can't carry it on the bike."

"Get your mom to bring it in the car sometime," Clare says. "And how about you bring Seraphina's hair over to my house?"

"I guess. But I'd have to hide it from Aunt Faye."

"That's not so hard. You can think of something."

"Yeah, just like you think of ways to meet Renzo." I tug on Clare's ponytail. "Better watch it. Your mom might get wild with the scissors if she finds out."

"Morgan! Don't even joke about that. Do you think I *want* to lie to Mom? Do you think I *like* deceiving her? I've never felt so guilty about anything in my life."

"Yeah, I know what you mean. You're *forced* to be bad!"

"Something like that." Clare glances around the loft. "Everything's okay here, so let's go. I'm getting hungry."

As we ride on, the temperature rises. Powdery dust from the gravel road coats the masses of tiger lilies and daisies and buttercups growing by the ditches. Dulcy's bike is too small and my whole body feels cramped. Meanwhile, the washboard road jolts me. But Clare looks totally content, her canvas shoes flashing pinkly as she pedals.

When we finally reach Cheltingdon Fairgrounds, we rest under the willows by the river and gulp from our water bottles. The lush green grass I remember from the day of the family picnic is now withered and brown. And there's no one fishing today. The muddy river is low, gunky with algae at the edges. A moldy smell rises from the surface.

It's not the best spot to eat lunch, but Clare doesn't want anybody to see us. "Mom has spies," she says. "Her friends in town — if any of them saw me with Renzo, they'd phone her right away."

We've just finished our sandwiches when Renzo appears. Clare jumps up, acting all surprised. "Renzo! What are you doing here?" As she flips back her visor, I can see the helpless, adoring look on her face.

Renzo laughs. "I'm on my lunch break. Just thought I'd take a walk." His voice sounds husky, almost as deep as Dulcy pretends with her Renzo doll. His eyes are dark and his hair curls in the most perfect way.

"Oh hey, what a coincidence," I say. "And we were just out for a nice innocent picnic."

Clare sits back down and motions for Renzo to sit beside her. They ignore me and talk together in low voices. She kind of leans into him and their fingers touch lightly. Her face glows with how she feels about him. I sit there wondering if Jeff Tan — or anybody else — will ever, ever, look at me the way Renzo is looking at Clare.

And then I have the urge to tell Mom about Clare's secret boyfriend. I mean, I don't mind helping Clare see Renzo, and I wouldn't want to mess things up for them. I just want Mom to know that Clare isn't so perfect. She's as sneaky as Mom says I am.

When I can't stand watching Clare and Renzo any longer, I crumple my lunch bag into a ball and hurl it at them. It flies straight between their heads. Jade herself couldn't have aimed better. They turn and gape like they've never seen me before.

"Anybody want another cookie?" I ask. When they look away, my fingers pretend to snip off Clare's hair.

In a little while Renzo says he has to go back to work. As he heads off across the fairgrounds towards town, Clare can't take her eyes off him. When he's almost out of sight, she says, "Hey, Morgan, want to go get ice cream? I brought some money."

"Sure!" But as we ride our bikes to the general store I realize that it's right beside Cordona's Hardware. So this is really just an excuse to follow Renzo. Well, who cares? I never turn down ice cream.

Sitting out on the steps of the store eating our cones, Clare says, "You know what? Maybe I won't tell Mom about the cabin after all."

"Oh yeah?" I lick at my dripping ice cream.

Clare hands me a paper napkin. "Yeah, I mean, she'd never find out it's been vandalized, she's way to busy to ever go over there herself. But mentioning it to her might tip her off, she might figure out my plan."

"And you don't want me to say anything either?" Clare's ice cream doesn't seem to be melting at all. What *is* it with her? How can she eat so neatly?

"Do you mind?"

I shrug. "As long as I don't actually have to lie to Aunt Faye."

"No, no, I'll do that," Clare says with a frustrated sigh. "I'm almost getting used to it."

We head home in the heat, not talking much. What if lying gets easier every time you do it? And what if, eventually, you *do* get used to it? "I'm sure not practising high jump tonight after all this biking," I say. "I'm beat. And I sure wish I'd brought more water."

"But seeing Renzo was worth it," Clare says, handing me her water bottle, which is still half-full. "Thanks for coming with me, Morgan."

"That's okay." But is it? What have I done, helping Clare and Renzo meet? I worry about it all the way back to the farm.

Grandma's gone out to dinner with Fergus, but she's left me a plate of mixed sandwiches with pickles, raw veggies and dip on the side. She's also left me a note. It says she'll be back by ten, and that Jade called.

7

I'M HOT AND HUNGRY AND TIRED AFTER THE BIKE RIDE WITH
Clare, but I phone Jade right away and she actually answers.
"Hey," she says. "Sorry I never called you back sooner, but
you know how it is."

"Yeah, yeah, I know. How *are* you? How's things in
Northington?"

"That's why I called," Jade says. "I saw that Arden chick
yesterday at Parker Pool. And she was wearing the sluttiest
bathing suit — I mean, ohmigod, even *I* wouldn't wear
something like that! And Jeff Tan was there too and I was
pretty sure you'd want to know."

"You think he likes her?"

"I can't see why — she's *such* a bitch. But everybody says
they're going together, and it sure looked that way. Oops, got
a beep, can you hold?"

I'm glad Grandma's not here to see my face as I wait for
Jade to take her other call. "Anyway," she says when she comes
back on the line, "I met this new guy? He's a friend of my
brother's? And he is *so* hot!"

"Sounds good." It's not even worth asking her more about
him. By next week Jade will be after some other guy. "So
how's Preston Paints doing?"

"Great! We played Westmore Plumbing last night and

beat them 12 to 3. I struck out five — but I sure miss you catching. Hey, any cute guys out there at the farm?"

"Well, my cousin has this boyfriend, Renzo. She's not allowed to see him, but she does anyway, and — "

"Sorry, another beep. Gotta go."

Jade hangs up. I guess I should be glad she called me at all, but I really wanted to talk to her about Clare and Renzo, to ask her if I should keep helping them get together. Jade knows way more about stuff like sex than I do. I've never even kissed a guy. Okay, I've never even held hands.

And now Jeff is going with Arden.

I run up to my room where I turn on the fan Grandma gave me and lie on my bed fuming. I'm too mad to cry. Jeff and Arden? *What is his problem?*

I whack at my pillow with my fists. I hate Arden! Not only did she take away my friends — now she's going with the only guy I've ever liked. And what's worse, even with all my practising, I'll probably never be able to beat her at high jump.

The fan whirs and cools me as I glare around Mom's old bedroom with its slanted ceiling and pine floor. I hate Mom too. So what if this room is comfy and charming? She can't make me stay a little girl by keeping me here. Going to Jade's party wasn't all that bad — not as bad as Clare trying to meet Renzo and *do it* with him in the old cabin.

Mom should be sorry she overreacted and stuck me at Grandma's. Maybe she already is. See, I'm still not really speaking to her.

If I happen to be here when Mom calls, I just say, *Yeah, hi, I'm fine.* I don't ask how she is or anything. Then when Mom tries to make me talk, I tell her, *Oh, sorry, gotta go now.*

Grandma needs to call Fergus. And hang up on her. Sort of like Jade did with me.

Well, maybe it's time to start speaking to Mom again. Time to tell her off. But not on the phone. I'm not brave enough for that. What I'll do is write Mom a letter. After all, she did give me notepaper and all those pre-stamped envelopes.

I go back downstairs and take my sandwiches out of the fridge. Before I left this morning I put one of the sports drinks Mom bought me in to chill, and I gulp it down before I eat. Then I devour my dinner as I think what to say.

Dear Mom,

Sorry I didn't write sooner but there's always so much else to do. Like gathering eggs and sewing quilt squares and watching the corn grow. You know. Anyway, you asked what's new. Nothing! Mostly I play dolls with Dulcy, which really makes me feel mature. I don't see much of Clare — she's got better things to do. So the summer sure is working out the way you planned.

Don't miss ya,

luv, Morgan

After that I take a long shower and get ready for bed. But before I go to sleep I sit staring out my window at Seraphina, holding the buckle half in my hand. Mom will be furious if she finds out I helped Clare see Renzo. And she'll go nuts if she finds out I agreed to keep quiet about the cabin. She'll be even madder than she was after Jade's party.

Are you sure you know what you're doing? Mom's voice asks. An anxious feeling worries its way through my whole body.

But Grandma helped Seraphina see Jed. So how bad can helping Clare be?

Bad, Mom's voice says.

*

Grandma is stirring something in her big canning kettle when I come downstairs the next morning. A sharp, spicy smell fills the kitchen.

"What's cooking, Gram?"

"Green tomato relish."

"Smells kinda strange."

Grandma sniffs the air and smiles. "Sweet and sour both. Fergus just loves it."

"Hmm." I pour myself a glass of juice and sit down at the table. "Gram, when my mother was a kid, was she ever bad?"

Grandma stops stirring and rubs her hands on her apron. "Well, of course," she says. "All kids are, sometimes."

"But what did she get in trouble for?"

"Well, let me think. One time she picked all Faye's watermelons before they could ripen. So she had to do Faye's morning chores for the rest of the summer."

"And what else did she do?"

"Lots. She was quite the little rebel, your mother. Funny she's so conservative now."

"That's for sure."

"She wouldn't like me telling you much. She'd think I was giving you ideas."

I finish my juice and serve myself some granola. "I suppose she told you all about Jade, and how she had to get me away from her."

"She might have mentioned it. Seemed a bit harsh, if you ask me." Grandma uses tongs to lift sterilized jars off a tray in the oven. "My girls are such worriers, now they've got teenaged daughters of their own. Give me a hand here?"

"Oh yeah. Maybe we should call them the Strict Sisters." Grandma bursts out laughing and I have to hold a jar steady while she ladles relish into it. "But that's why you should tell me, Gram — so I'll understand her better."

"Well." Grandma nods towards the next jar. "Let's see. She was furious once when I wouldn't let her stay overnight at a party in town."

"How old was she?"

"Oh, about fifteen, I guess. She thought she was all grown up, anyway." Grandma pats her hair, which the steam from the relish is twisting into funny little curls.

"Go on, Gram."

"She had to gather the eggs every day, just like you do. The morning of the party her basket didn't have near as many eggs as usual. That's all there were, she told me."

"And then what?"

"Well, you know how those hens can be. Hiding the eggs and trying to keep you from them. So later I went out to check. I thought maybe she'd just missed some. But there weren't any more eggs in the nests, or anywhere else in the henhouse. I couldn't figure it out. Then after supper I took a bowl of peelings to the compost heap behind the barn. And what did I see?"

"What?"

"Eggs. Smashed and splattered all over the back of the barn. About a dozen she'd heaved at the wall."

"Hah! What did you do?"

"When it came time to give out allowances, I had enough money for Faye's, but not for your mother's. I hadn't sold enough eggs, I told her. And we never spoke of it again."

"Oh, I can hardly believe it! My perfect mother!"

"Nobody's perfect, Morgan." Grandma fills the last jar, wipes down the stovetop and counter. "Now why don't you run along and gather today's eggs?"

A nasty little plan creeps into my head as I hurry out to the henhouse. The chickens fuss and squawk as I dig into the nests under them for their warm brown eggs. *Don't even think about it,* Mom's voice warns. *You know it's not a good idea.*

Still, I head out behind the barn to have a look. Am I imagining things, or can I really see dark stains slopped up and down the wall?

I set down my basket.

I take an egg in my hand, just to get the feel of it. Like all the others, it's spattered with bits of straw and manure. Well then, one less to wash. I choose a spot on the wall and pretend it's Mom's head.

I pull my arm back.

The egg goes flying!

"That's for ruining my summer," I say, watching an oozy yellow mess drip down the wall.

I throw the next egg hard and low, like when I want to pick off a runner stealing second. Splat! Got her! She's out!

"And that's for — "

"Morgan?" Grandma's voice calls from the house. "Morgan, Dulcy's here."

Careful to keep the rest of the eggs from breaking, I rush back to the kitchen. As I set the basket on the counter, Grandma gives me a funny look. But she doesn't say a word.

I dash back outside to find Dulcy sitting at the edge of Seraphina's Circle, combing the long grass. "Clare showed me how to make a French braid," she says. "She did her hair that way last night, because she was going out with Renzo. But she told Mom she was going over to Nicole's house. Nicole came and picked her up."

Did Clare meet Renzo at the cabin? Probably. *You should tell your aunt about that,* I hear Mom say. *Should* I tell somebody? Like maybe Grandma — she'd know what to do.

But Clare trusted me with her secret. I can't rat her out. That's what somebody like Arden would do. What am I supposed to do? I want to be a good friend to Clare, but I don't want anything bad to happen to her. I wish she'd never told me about Renzo. Then this wouldn't be my problem.

8

DULCY AND I WORK AT UNBRAIDING ALL THE GRASS, AND then we go into Seraphina's Circle. I keep thinking about throwing those eggs at the barn wall, and how good it felt. I've never understood kids who like to vandalize, but now maybe I do. There's something so satisfying about smashing stuff. Yeah, yeah, I know what Mom would say about that. Well, so what?

"Clare looked really beautiful last night when she went with Nicole to meet Renzo!" Dulcy says, picking up her dolls. "Oh, but these are getting all brown and shrivelled up. Should we make new ones?" She sets them aside while she gathers the dead wildflowers from around the dolls' house and sets out the new bouquets she's brought.

I take my Jeff and Leigh dolls down from the boughs. Dulcy is right — they are all dried up now. They don't look fresh and fun anymore. "That purple flower's poison, you know," I say.

"I know. It's nightshade, but just the berries are poison, not the flowers. Anyway, I think it looks pretty." Dulcy fiddles with the bouquet she's put in Clare and Renzo's living room. "What are you making with those sticks?"

"A high jump. It's time to teach Arden a lesson."

"But I thought you changed her name to Leigh?"

"I did, but I'm tired of playing with Leigh, so I changed it back." I poke two forked sticks into the earth and set another stick across them. I make my Arden doll try to jump over. Arden nicks the pole, knocking it right down. Her little cornhusk bonnet falls off. "See, she's not as good as she thinks she is," I say. "She hasn't been practising, she's been too busy with Jeff."

Darcy giggles. I set up the sticks again, remembering Jade's phone call. *Everybody says they're going together.* This time I don't even pretend to make Arden jump, I just crash her right through. "What a loser!" I shout.

And then suddenly I'm tearing my dolls apart, throwing the shredded husks of Jeff and Arden/Leigh all around Seraphina's Circle.

"Morgan!" Dulcy's voice is shrill. "What are you doing?"

"Trashing Jeff and Arden, what does it look like?"

"It looks like fun!" Dulcy makes her dolls face each other. "They're having their first fight!" she cries. "Renzo doesn't like Clare's French braid." She laughs in a funny, high-pitched cackle as she rips them apart. "Clare says she'll wear her hair however she wants, and she's never speaking to him again as long as she lives."

Dulcy flings the husks every which way just as I did. Then she looks around, confused. "But we're going to make new dolls," she says. "Aren't we, Morgan?"

I stare at what's left of the old ones. I can't believe I just did that. I mean, how messed up am I? I just attacked and destroyed some harmless dolls. In front of Dulcy. *And I enjoyed it.* Which proves it isn't good for me being at the farm. *It's making me crazy.*

"I don't know," I say.

*

After Dulcy goes home, I feel worse and worse about the ruined dolls. Yeah, it felt good at the time, just like the eggs, but now it makes me sick. I decide I have to do something nice to make up for my behaviour. "Want me to get dinner ready, Grandma?" I offer. She's been in the hot kitchen all day — when she finished her relish, she started a big batch of pickles and baked three lemon loaves.

She looks surprised. I haven't helped her out much, just stuffed my face with her good cooking. "Oh, that would be lovely, Morgan," she says. "I'll take the newspaper and a glass of lemonade and go relax in my lawn chair."

I'm not much of a cook, but there's some cold chicken in the fridge, and I boil some new potatoes to go with it. I slice some tomatoes and make a green salad, and then I even pick a bouquet of snapdragons for the table.

Once we've eaten, I ask, "Gram, when you were a kid and you helped Seraphina meet Jed, were you ever scared? I mean, did you ever worry about what you were doing? Did you ever think it was wrong?"

"You sure have a lot of questions today." Grandma starts clearing the table. "And you made dinner — is there something you want to tell me?"

"Oh no," I say, blushing. "I'm just curious, is all." I scrape my plate and stack it in the dishwasher. "It's such a romantic story."

Grandma covers the leftover salad. "Yes, it is, isn't it? I suppose that's why I helped her." She puts the salad in the fridge and sets out one of the freshly baked lemon loaves. "I was only Dulcy's age, and it all seemed so exciting. And Seraphina was like a mother to me, so I listened to her and did what she told me to do."

"Everything?" I slice two large pieces off the lemon loaf. "You did everything she told you?

"No thanks, dear," Grandma says as I offer her a slice of lemon loaf. "Yes, everything. I wasn't sorry until later. And then of course, after Seraphina died, well, I was just devastated with guilt. And terrified of what Father might do to me."

"And what did he do?" Like I don't already know. But I want to hear it again anyway.

Grandma closes her eyes a minute. "He punished me with silence," she says with a deep frown. "Our neighbour Mrs. Laing moved in to look after us, since she was a widow without children of her own. And Father never spoke directly to me again."

"Not even on your wedding day," I add. "He wouldn't come to your wedding. Your brother had to walk you down the aisle."

"Not even on my wedding day." Grandma gets up to put the kettle on for tea. "And that was fifteen years later. Heavens, I was twenty-five, almost a spinster in those days. You'd think he'd be glad to have me married off, but he bore a grudge till the day he died. Carried it right to the grave."

"So you and Grandpa Duncan lived in town until your father died, and then you moved back here."

"Yes, my brothers all had land of their own by then. And Mrs. Laing's nephew, who was Uncle Paul's father, took over her farm."

I finish my first slice of lemon loaf and start on the next.

"Tell me again about the day Seraphina died."

Grandma takes her time making and pouring the tea. "Well," she finally says, "it was the middle of February. Seraphina hadn't seen Jed since Christmas. It was much harder to arrange things in the winter. I couldn't just run over there any old time. The snow was far too deep. So we had to make another plan."

"You pretended to be sick," I say between bites, "so she'd have to take the cutter over to the Laing farm for help. It was so long ago you didn't even have a car or a phone."

"No," Grandma says, "we didn't have a car or a phone because we were too poor. But Mrs. Laing, who was a nurse, had both. We always went to her for medical advice and home remedies. Since Seraphina had fallen in love with Jed, that was the only reason Father would let anyone go over there."

"But he didn't believe you when you said you felt ill."

"No, he didn't trust us. But when he went out to the barn to do the chores, Seraphina fed me honey, then gave me warm salt water to drink so I'd vomit. I stuck my finger down my throat to help things along. She wrapped me in blankets and a hot water bottle, so I'd look feverish. When he came in, I clutched at my side and doubled over in pretend pain. We made it look like appendicitis, which could be fatal in those days. The idea was that Mrs. Laing would know whether to call the doctor in Plattsworth."

"And you knew Mrs. Laing was out on Wednesday afternoons at the church women's group. So while Seraphina waited for Mrs. Laing to come home, she could be with Jed." I swallow my last bite of lemon loaf and lick my fingers. "Mmm, that was so good, Gram. But weren't you afraid she'd know you were faking? I mean, if Mrs. Laing was a nurse."

"Oh no," Grandma says. "We knew it was possible to have a sudden appendix attack which didn't develop into appendicitis. We figured I could have several attacks over the next few weeks."

"And always on Wednesdays."

We both laugh at that, and then, suddenly, we both stop. After all, there had been no more Wednesdays for Seraphina.

"So," Grandma continues, "because I looked so sick, Father let Seraphina go to Mrs. Laing's. He even hitched up our old horse Maude to the cutter for her."

"And then you waited." I play with the crumbs on my plate. "And waited and waited."

Grandma nods, her eyes filling up with tears. "Pretty soon the sky clouded over and it started to snow. By late afternoon, when she still wasn't back, Father wanted to go looking for her, but by then it was a real blizzard." Grandma stops to dry her eyes and blow her nose. "I got terrified and told him everything. I didn't have to pretend to be sick anymore. I really was. Heartsick. Something awful had happened to her, and it was all my fault."

"No," I say. "Not your fault at all. It was an accident."

"But she couldn't have gone if I hadn't helped her."

I think of Clare and her plans, and a pang of guilt stabs me. My heart shivers, and I can't sit still. I start pacing around the kitchen while Grandma talks. "We had to wait hours for the storm to be over. By dawn the wind had dropped, though it was still snowing. And sometime during the night, Maude had come back, alone. So Father put on his snowshoes and set out to look for Seraphina. A few hours later he came home and told us she was dead."

Grandma's voice has gone all weak and trembly. I stop my

pacing behind her and circle her with a hug. I've never heard Grandma tell the story like this, as if it just happened.

Grandma clasps my hands in hers. "The cutter had gone into the ditch when Seraphina made the turn up the lane between our road and the Laing farm. She was thrown under it and broke her leg. Somehow she managed to free Maude, but she couldn't save herself."

And I know exactly where that happened. The place where Dulcy and I used to leave wildflowers when we acted out Seraphina's life. When Clare played Seraphina. "Stop, Gram," I say softly. For the first time the story is so real I can't bear to listen to the end. "Don't tell the rest, it's too awful."

But Grandma doesn't seem to hear. She goes to the sideboard and lifts out the stationery box. She opens it gently. Then she takes out Seraphina's hair and stands there stroking it. "My beautiful sister froze to death," she says. "When Father found her, Seraphina was buried in snow."

9

MOM PHONES AS SOON AS SHE GETS MY LETTER. BUT WHEN the phone rings, I'm about to leave for the Laing farm with some of Grandma's pickles and relish, and I don't feel like talking anyway. So I say, "Tell her I'll call back, okay Gram?" Then I somehow keep forgetting to do it.

A few days later Grandma brings a letter for me in from the mailbox. She doesn't comment, just tucks it under my plate at breakfast. It's from Mom — like I didn't see *that* coming. I turn the envelope over and over in my hands, imagining her words. But I don't even need to open it to know what she'll say. I stick the letter in my pocket with the buckle half and go outside.

I try to practise high jump. But the letter is bulky and makes a scrunching noise that distracts me. Finally I give up and creep into Seraphina's circle. I haven't wanted to come here since the day I trashed the cornhusk dolls. The sight of them now makes me feel sick.

And then I want Mom so much that I plunk down in the middle of the mess and start to read her letter.

Dear Morgan,

Please realize parents have certain responsibilities. One is doing what they think best, whether their children like it or not. I'm sorry Clare's so busy — I did hope you could spend time with her. She's a lovely girl. But I still think staying at the farm will be good for you. Why not relax and keep an open mind? Who knows what might happen?

There's more, about Dad's golfing, and the upstairs bathroom Mom's renovating and the great time Glen is having at camp. But I barely skim those parts.

I guess I was really hoping Mom would see from my letter that her plan wasn't working and that she'd let me come home. I should have known better. Mom will never change her mind.

I want to talk to Jade, so I go inside and phone her. But of course I just get her voice mail. Too bad. She'd know just how I feel. If she answered she'd make me laugh, doing her best imitation of my mother's voice and mannerisms.

But what I really need is to see Jade. To play softball with her. She could make me forget everything with her fantastic pitching. She'd throw so fast I wouldn't be able to think of anything but catching. The ball would smack into my glove so hard my hand would sting for an hour afterwards.

But Jade isn't here. And I'm not there.

When Dulcy comes over later, she takes one look at me and says, "What happened to you?"

"Nothing. I'm fine."

"C'mon," Dulcy says. "Let's make new dolls. Then you'll feel better."

"No, I won't. Those dolls are for babies. I can't believe we ever played with them."

"It was fun." Now it's Dulcy who looks like she's going to cry. "I loved playing with them."

"Yeah, I know," I say. "Sorry. But just not today, okay? We'll make new dolls soon, I promise." Maybe Dulcy will forget about the dolls, the way she seems to have forgotten about the half of Seraphina's buckle. "Let's practise high jump. It's pretty hot, but athletes have to work hard no matter what."

All that week I avoid making the new dolls by pretending I'm getting ready for the all-star meet. "I've got to train harder," I tell Dulcy as I set up my stuff each day. "See how much better we're both getting?" Dulcy can make 1 metre now. I can jump 1.37 easily and I've jumped 1.4 twice. If I can only clear 1.45 at the all-star meet, I know I can win. My goal is in sight.

*

On Sunday morning, Clare calls. "Mom wants you and Grandma to come over for dinner," she says. "Don't forget to bring Seraphina's hair to show me."

"Oh." I'm not sure I want to see that hair again. But how can I refuse? "Well, okay. I guess I could bring it in my backpack."

For Sunday dinner Uncle Paul barbeques whole chickens which Aunt Faye serves with early corn. After we eat, the adults sit on the verandah while the kids play ball on the big front lawn. The Bees are amazing. They all have good arms and can hit almost any pitch.

After a while Uncle Paul joins the game. He stands beside me in the outfield, looking as relaxed and happy as I've seen him all summer.

"Uncle Paul?" I say as we wait for Clare to find a foul ball hit into the ditch. "Do you think you could teach me to drive the tractor tonight?"

"Nope." Uncle Paul catches a fly ball hit by Dulcy. "Yer out!" he yells. "Batter's out!"

I try to smile as if I don't really care. "Okay, well, thanks anyway."

"But I don't mind giving you a first lesson." He pushes me out of the way so I miss an easy grounder. "City kid out here," he calls to my cousins. "Can't catch worth a darn!"

"Hey thanks, Uncle Paul!" Who cares if he insults my catching? "Thanks a million, billion, trillion!"

When the game is over and the Bees are busy watering the vegetable garden, Uncle Paul calls me. "Come on then, Morgan. You probably won't be able to do it, but you can give it a try." He leads me down to the barnyard.

The old tractor must have been painted orange once, but now it's almost pure rust. A thick piece of foam is strapped to the saucer-like metal seat to make it more comfortable. The seat is big enough for both of us.

I sit in front of Uncle Paul. Then suddenly he flicks the key and the whole tractor rumbles and shakes. "Gears tend to jam," he yells over the racket, "so start her in the gear you want."

All the knobs and levers look the same to me. "Uncle Paul! I don't know what you mean!" I grip the steering wheel as if it might fly away.

"Clutch in to start, clutch out, she goes. Don't shift. She gets stuck."

"Wait!" I scream as we begin to roll. "Stop! I don't get it!"

But Uncle Paul can't, or won't, hear me. We lurch across the barnyard towards the back lane.

I cling to the wheel in terror. The seat bounces up and

down with each bump and rut. And then I see we're headed straight for the barnyard gate.

"Help!" My hands leave the wheel to cover my head. "We're going to crash!"

Uncle Paul grabs the wheel and turns it sharply, almost tipping the tractor over. "Gotta steer her," he calls into my ear as we start back down the lane.

At last he stops the tractor. "Reckon that's enough for now?"

My stomach flip-flops and my legs feel like jelly as I climb off. "Thanks, Uncle Paul," I make myself say. "That was so fun!"

I sort of stumble back to the house, where everyone is still on the verandah, relaxing in the cool evening air.

"Let's go upstairs," Clare says.

"Nah. It'll be too hot and stuffy inside." I just want to sit safely by Grandma for a while.

"Oh, come on up. I have to check on the Bees. They never settle down." Clare mouths the word *Renzo* at me, then puts her hands together as if she's praying. I know what she means is: *please, please.*

After we look in on the Bees, who are having a pillow fight, we rest on our stomachs on the twin beds in Clare and Dulcy's room. I lie beside Dulcy, facing the wide open window.

There isn't a bit of breeze. Through the white ruffled curtains, just like those in my room at Grandma's, I can see a few faint stars and a pale sliver of moon.

"Did you bring it?" Clare asks.

I point to my backpack on the floor.

"Bring what?" Dulcy demands.

"Seraphina's hair," Clare says, digging around in my pack. "Great-grandfather Hamish chopped it off, and Grandma kept it all these years."

Dulcy watches, speechless, as Clare opens the box and shows her the hair. "Oh, it's so pretty," she cries, after I fill in the details. "But it's so creepy too, I mean, it's almost like we're really seeing her."

Clare lifts the hair out and holds it up beside her own. The colour is almost identical. "It feels so real," she says. "You're right, Dulcy, it's like she's right here with us."

"You look just like that photo of her." Dulcy reaches up to touch the hair. "Hey, you could actually be Seraphina, just like Grandma always says."

"Okay, give it back now." I hold out my hands. I can't bear to see Clare holding that hair. And what if it reminds Dulcy about finding the bit of buckle? "Our mothers aren't supposed to know we've seen it," I say. "What if Aunt Faye comes up here? We better put it away." I want to hide that hair forever. "Hey, only two weeks till the all-star track meet," I say, stuffing the box into my backpack. "I can hardly wait."

"I'm really sorry I can't come with you and Dulcy," Clare says. "But Dad needs a lot of extra help. Summer's his busiest time."

"I know, I know, that's okay." I tiptoe to the door and close it, even though that will make the room even hotter. "So what about Renzo?" I don't mention the cabin because of Dulcy, who'd never be able to keep something like that to herself.

"I've got an idea," Clare says. "Renzo can't phone here, in case Mom or Dad answers, so it's really hard to make arrangements to meet. And he never works the same hours, so we can't go by that. But I was thinking, if he phoned you at Grandma's, then you could give me his messages."

My insides knot up. "Why doesn't he just email you?"

"Mom might see it. And you know she likes the computer to be used only for farm business."

"Well, why doesn't he call your friend Nicole?"

"Because Nicole's got a summer job in Plattsworth, and she's never home. And anyway, Mom might suspect Nicole, but she'd never suspect you."

"Don't you think Grandma might?" I pull at a thread unravelling from Dulcy's patchwork quilt. "I don't get many phone calls, except from my mother. Who would I say it was?"

"Tell her it's some guy from Northington who's got a crush on you."

"Like, duh — there aren't any."

"Make one up. Pretend it's somebody you wish would call."

I pull the thread all the way out and snap it off. "You mean like Jeff Tan?" I wrap the thread around my finger to make a ring. "Okay, I guess I could do that."

"Oh, thank you, thank you!" Clare jumps up to give me a hug. "You're the best, Morgan!"

"Yeah, right." I roll the thread ring off, letting it drop to the floor. "The very best. I have a fake boyfriend, and I was scared to death on that tractor."

Clare laughs. "I bet Jeff Tan likes you," she says. "How could he not?"

"Because of Arden?" I say. "Oh man, I so don't want to see her at the all-star meet. But anyway, tell me, how *do* you drive that tractor?"

"Oh, it's just plain stubborn." Clare shakes her head and laughs. "You have to be tough with it. Show it who's boss."

"Yeah?"

"Sure. I just whip that wheel around and give it the gas."

"I don't think I can learn. I'm only good at one thing, and that's high jump."

"Softball too," Dulcy says. "And you're lots of fun to play with."

I picture the shredded dolls in Seraphina's Circle. Why didn't I at least stop Dulcy from ruining her dolls too? Oh, I am *such* a loser. And now I've gone and agreed to getting Clare into even more trouble with Renzo.

The room has grown steadily darker, but we haven't turned on any lights. Soon Grandma calls from downstairs that it's time to go. Dulcy, who is falling asleep right where she is, mumbles something about tomorrow.

A sort of sadness sighs from the shadows. I shudder as it clouds around me like a fog. Then I push myself free. I'm just spooked because of that tractor ride. "See you guys," I say, making my voice cheery and bright.

Clare tucks a pillow under Dulcy's head. She smiles as I leave the room, waving a silent goodbye.

10

THE PHONE RINGS FIRST THING MONDAY MORNING. FOR A minute I hope it might be Jade, but of course it isn't. The call *is* for me though. Grandma answers, and I can tell by the look on her face that it's not Dulcy. "Sounds male," she says, handing me the phone with a wink.

Please, let it not be Renzo. But it is.

"Hey, Morgan," his deep voice says. "Can you tell Clare I've got tonight off? She should tell her parents she's coming over to visit you, okay?"

"Oh hi," I say. "How's things in Northington?"

Renzo laughs. "I'll pick Clare up at the end of the back lane and drop her off there later."

"I'm fine, thanks." Do I sound fake? I'm sure sweating. But Grandma's busy at the sink, making a point of not watching me. "Yeah, it's great here at the farm."

"And can you cover for us if Clare's Mom calls there tonight to check?"

No! I've changed my mind. I don't want to do this. "That's right, I'm coming home for the all-star meet. I can't wait."

"Call Clare's mom at nine-thirty," Renzo says. "Tell her Clare just left to walk home. Okay?"

"Okay. Well, thanks for calling, Jeff. I'll see you soon." My hand is shaking as I hang up. I've never actually talked to Jeff Tan on the phone in my life. Did I fool Grandma?

"Somebody special?" she asks.

I flash her a girlfriend grin. "Maybe," I say as I rush outside to set up my high-jump stuff. Practising always helps me burn off stress. And I am feeling super stressed right now.

What if something goes wrong? What if Renzo can't drop Clare off on time? What if we all get caught? Mom would totally freak. Ohmigod, then she might not even let me come home for the all-star meet!

I spend the evening watching a crime show on tape with Grandma, trying to hide what a nervous wreck I am over Clare's date. On TV they always figure everything out, sooner or later. I'm sure Mom or Aunt Faye will too. Eventually they'll put all the clues together, and they'll know what's going on.

I can't even eat the popcorn Grandma makes us. "You must really like that guy who called," she says. "Loss of appetite is a sure sign."

"What?" The smell of the melted butter, which I usually love, makes me want to throw up. "Oh, um, yeah, I do kind of like him. But it's nothing serious, Gram. Guess I just ate too much at dinner is all."

"Hmm," Grandma says. "Seems to me you didn't eat a thing."

When I go to bed, instead of sleeping I just keep fretting. But the plan works fine. Clare calls the next morning to thank me. "We went to the cabin for awhile," she says, her voice all gooey, "and then we went for ice cream. I got home just in time. Mom was out in the yard watching for me."

"Great." At least somebody was having fun last night. And I can't help wondering what kind of fun. Were they making out? Did they do more than that? But I can hardly ask her with Grandma a few feet away pretending not to listen.

*

It's a week before Renzo calls again. This time Grandma asks in a teasing voice, "And who was that?"

"Oh, just this guy from home." My voice sounds innocent, like it's no big deal at all. Like I actually believe myself. "His name's Jeff Tan."

"And he's calling you again?" Grandma actually smirks at me. "Long distance? In the morning?"

"He has a phone plan, just like you." My suspicion that lying gets easier was right. I see now how easily lies slip out once you get started. "You have a boyfriend, Gram, so why shouldn't I?"

"Heavens, I never said you shouldn't." Grandma picks up the laundry basket by the back door. "Course, your mother might have a different opinion." She laughs as if that's the funniest thing. "Better hang this wash out. You get yourself some breakfast."

As soon as the door closes, I phone Clare to tell her Renzo's plans.

"Oh no!" Clare says. "Not this afternoon — I have to help Dad in the east field."

"Should I call Renzo back?"

"No, no, don't do that." Clare sounds desperate. "Maybe I can get it done this morning, if I really hurry. Yeah, I'm pretty sure I can."

"Okay." The thought of Aunt Faye ever finding out what's going on makes me squirm. To make myself feel better I say,

"Tell Dulcy to come over this afternoon, and we'll work on some new dolls."

Then I toast some cheese bread, but I can't eat it. My stomach is already full — full of guilt. And the rest of me is full of high-jump jitters. The all-star meet is only five days away.

The only thing I can do is practise. That always settles me down. As I start stretching, I try to block Renzo and Clare from my mind and concentrate on what I have to do to win. I close my eyes and visualize myself making 1.45 on Saturday. I see myself flying up and over the pole, right into the sky.

Then when I start jumping, power surges through me. My training is paying off. I jump higher and higher, full of strength. And when I finally set the pole at 1.45, I soar over on my first try. Woo-hoo!

Collapsing on the landing mat, I kick my feet in the air like a tickled baby. I am *so* ready. Now if I can only stay calm and focused.

I strut into the kitchen for a drink of water. How can I stay confident? How can I pass all the hours and hours between now and Saturday? Dulcy will be over later, but what to do till then?

I decide to read for a while. A good book will distract me, keep me from obsessing about Arden or worrying about Renzo and Clare.

It's almost noon, and I'm deep into a fantasy novel set in another world and time, when the phone rings again.

I ignore it. It's sure to be Dulcy, interrupting the story just when things are getting exciting. I hear Grandma answer and I read on. Probably she'll just take a message for me.

But then I hear Grandma hurrying upstairs. And then

she's bursting into my room calling, "Morgan, Morgan, oh Morgan." Her face looks like the end of the world. "I'm afraid there's some very bad news."

I drop my book. "What?"

"That was Uncle Paul."

"Uncle Paul?" He never phones. "What's happened?"

"An accident. A terrible accident." Grandma takes a deep breath, wiping her hands on her apron as if she wants to rub her skin right off. "That old tractor, it went out of control, she must have been going too fast and — "

"And what?"

"And Clare was driving, you see."

"*And?*"

"And it went into the ditch and she fell underneath it." Grandma's words fill every bit of space in the room.

I leap up and into her arms. Grandma holds me tight, moaning, "Oh Lord, oh Lord," over and over and over.

"Was she hurt badly, Gram?" I finally manage to ask.

Grandma's arms slacken. "Yes," she whispers, "she was." Grandma's body seems to crumple and shrink. "Her legs were crushed. Paul somehow managed, I don't know how, he got the tractor off her. But she, she also hit her head on a big rock. She's unconscious."

"Oh Gram! Has she gone to the hospital?"

"By ambulance, didn't you hear the sirens? They've taken her over to Plattsworth — Faye rode with her, and Paul's following in the car."

"I was reading. I didn't hear a thing!" I run to the window, as if looking out could change what's happened. "But she'll be okay, won't she?"

"Morgan," Grandma says. "Child, we don't really know.

We're just hoping and praying."

We hold each other again, then Grandma says, "She lost a lot of blood, she's gone into shock. The ambulance took almost half an hour to get there."

"What should we do?" I cry. "Is there anything we can do?"

"I've called your parents. They're on their way."

The floor falls out from under me. "My mom and dad are coming?" That can mean only one thing. *This is really, really serious.*

"Dulcy and the Bees are on their way over here." Grandma pulls a tissue from her apron pocket, takes off her glasses and dabs at her eyes. "Why don't you go on out and meet them?"

I don't want to. But maybe if I act normal it will help Grandma feel better. "Okay. Good idea."

11

AFTER GRANDMA LEAVES MY ROOM I TAKE THE BIT OF
Seraphina's buckle from my pocket. Closing my fingers
around it, I press it into my palm until my skin stings. I
absolutely have to give it to Dulcy today.

I head outside and see my cousins coming down the road.
The Bees are darting down into the ditch, out into the middle
of the road, down into the ditch again. I can almost hear
them buzzing. Dulcy is walking slowly behind with her head
bent, scuffing her feet in the gravel. She doesn't look up until
I call to her. Then she breaks into a run.

She runs right into my arms. "Oh, oh, oh," she wails. "It's
so awful. Her legs, oh her legs were all bleeding and I even
saw her bones and oh, oh, oh!"

The Bees don't speak. They just hover like I'm some
alien flower they've never seen before. Then they zoom away
towards the barn.

I take Dulcy straight to the edge of Seraphina's Circle.
I need to keep us both busy while we wait for word about
Clare. "We should braid the grass," I say. "We didn't do it last
time." That was the day we wrecked the dolls.

"I don't feel like it," Dulcy says.

"Neither do I. But we have to get the grass ready. We want
it to be all nice and wavy when we make our new dolls."

"Do you promise we're going to?" Dulcy sniffles and wipes at her nose. "Not today, but as soon as Clare's better?"

"Of course." I kneel and begin to comb the grass, separating it into strands for braiding. Dulcy does the same.

"Don't worry," I say as we work. "She'll be all right. They have doctors who can fix anything." I'm not exactly sure about that. But Dulcy looks so pathetic with her eyes rubbed red from crying and her hair straggling out of its purple plastic barrette that I have to say something hopeful.

"She lost so much blood though," Dulcy says with a sob, "waiting for the ambulance to come. Maybe they won't be able to fix her." She weaves the grass into a neat, tight braid, as if that can somehow save Clare.

"Sure they will. They'll give her transfusions."

"How do you know?"

"Because my Dad gives blood sometimes. He told me all about how donated blood can save lives."

"But Mom thinks Clare is going to die."

"No, she doesn't!"

"Yes she does. I heard her say so. She said Clare could die of shock."

I stop braiding. "Aunt Faye's just worried and upset and all that." I try to sound certain. I try not to think about my parents coming. "Clare's going to be fine. Maybe she'll have to be in the hospital for a while, but she'll get better."

"Do you really think so? Mom said the head injury might make her, you know, not ever okay again. Even if her legs are."

Brain damage? I never even thought about that. "She'll be fine! Of course she will!"

Then Grandma is calling us for lunch. "C'mon, let's go

eat." Not that I'm hungry, but we've finished with the grass, and there's no way I want Dulcy going inside Seraphina's Circle where the ruined dolls are.

Grandma has a big plate of sandwiches and carrot sticks and a tin of cookies ready for us. She starts pouring glasses of milk, and jokes to the boys, "I bet you Bees want some nice nectar for lunch!" She's trying so hard to make everything seem normal. But the only time I've ever seen Grandma's face look like that was when she told me about Seraphina's death.

The Bees eat like they haven't been fed for weeks. Dulcy picks at her food, pulling the sandwiches apart and breaking the carrot sticks into bits. But Grandma and I don't eat anything at all.

"Go on, Morgan, you need some food," Grandma says. "You didn't have much breakfast."

"I'm not really hungry."

The Bees poke each other and mess around as if nothing is wrong. One of them puts carrot sticks in his mouth like fangs. Another sticks some up his nose. They all laugh. Even Dulcy gives a weak little smile.

For the first time in my life, I feel more like an adult than a kid.

After lunch Dulcy and I go back outside. "Let's sit in Seraphina's Circle," Dulcy says.

"Nah."

"Oh please, Morgan?"

"Sorry, Dulcy. I just don't feel like it." What I really want is to be alone, not to have to talk to anyone. Especially not Dulcy.

"How about high jump then?"

"*No!*"

"Well, what do you want to do?"

"I want to go for a walk. By myself! I want you to get lost." I start to run away. "Buzz off. Go play with the Bees."

"Sorry, sorry," I hear Dulcy call, but I don't stop and I don't look back.

I run past the barn and down the lane that leads to Grandma's sugar bush. I keep going until my chest aches and my legs burn. And then, thinking about Clare's legs, I force myself to run farther.

Finally I slow down a little. *Please, please, let Clare be okay,* my mind begs. But who am I asking? God? I don't really know. Grandma mentioned prayers, but I'm not sure that's enough.

Please God, I try anyway, *please don't let Clare die. I'll do anything, God, I promise. I'll let Arden win at the all-star meet. I'll be nicer to Dulcy. I'll even be nicer to Mom. But please, please, let Clare live.*

I kind of stumble on until I reach the shade of the woods. An overgrown path leads me to the clearing where the sugar shanty stands. Sunlight through the maple leaves spreads lacy shadows all around. I sit on a stump and catch my breath.

Then I think of Dulcy, probably sitting all alone in Seraphina's Circle, surrounded by the shredded cornhusk dolls. I'm such a jerk for deserting her. I should run straight back and apologize. And also return the bit of buckle.

But I can't.

My throat dry and aching, I just sit there. Why was Clare hurt? What if she dies? What if she's in a coma for years and years and years? And what if she wakes up and lives, but she can't walk and she's not right in the head?

It shouldn't have happened. It doesn't make sense. It isn't fair.

And what about Renzo? I suddenly remember he'll be waiting for Clare at the end of the lane. Probably he'll stick around for a while, then figure she couldn't get away and go on home. He won't know what happened. He'll think Clare is just fine.

And then an even worse thought strikes me. If I hadn't helped Renzo set up the meeting, maybe Clare wouldn't have gotten hurt. That tractor's difficult to handle. If she hadn't been in such a hurry she might have driven more carefully.

It's all my fault!

I fish the piece of Seraphina's buckle from my pocket.

Staring at it, I think about my great-aunt and how she died. I think about Grandma's part in that, how she only wanted to help. I think about how I only wanted to help. Then I cry and cry and cry.

If only I could change places with Clare.

I'm the one who's bad.

I'm the one who deserves to be hurt.

I'm the one who should be lying there in the hospital.

*

The sun hangs low in the sky by the time I wander back down the lane. I didn't realize it was so late — I sure hope Grandma isn't worried. In the distance I can see dust rising along the gravel road. That means a car is coming. As I reach the farmhouse, my parents' old station wagon is pulling into the lane.

I race to meet them. "Mom!" Forget not speaking to her. Tears of relief are streaming down my cheeks as I shout,

"Mom! Oh Mom, I'm so glad to see you!"

Mom doesn't say anything. She just hugs me longer and harder than she ever has before.

"Can we go straight to the hospital?" My voice comes out all shaky.

"Yes, I think we'd better." Mom's voice sounds even shakier. "I'll just go in and see Grandma for a minute first."

But before she can, Grandma steps out onto the back porch. She bends to set down a pan of bread and milk for the barn cats, who come scampering from all directions. "Faye just called," she says when she straightens. "Clare's out of surgery but she hasn't regained consciousness yet. And she's still in intensive care, so only her parents can visit."

12

MOURNING DOVES COO SOFTLY OUTSIDE MY WINDOW, JUST as they always do. But today it seems like the most depressing sound I've ever heard.

It can't be true.

Clare can't be in hospital in critical condition.

It's totally impossible.

But that's what Aunt Faye and Uncle Paul told us last night when they came to pick up Dulcy and the Bees. Clare had over six hours of surgery on her legs and a lot of blood transfusions. She's still in a coma, which means she's so unconscious she's not responding to voices or touch or anything.

After the Laings left, Grandma and Mom and Dad and I sat around for hours crying and trying to console each other. Then I lay awake all night, full of guilt and grief, trying to understand.

Still dazed, I drag myself out of bed and over to the window. Why is the world still there? How dare it be? Didn't it end yesterday?

But no, *it's not the end of the world,* that's what the grownups said. They said *there's still hope, and we have to cling to that.* I stare across the flat fields. Dad once explained to me how millions of years ago this land was the bottom of a great inland sea. I can feel the weight of all that water washing over me, dragging me down. Drowning me in hot salty tears.

Downstairs, my parents and Grandma speak in hushed voices. No one eats breakfast. I climb onto my mother's lap, something I haven't done for years.

"Are they going to move Clare?" I ask. My words sound like sobs, and I feel fresh tears coming. Yesterday the doctors wanted to transfer Clare to Sick Kids. But then Aunt Faye and Uncle Paul couldn't visit her, because they can't leave the farm for more than a few hours. Neighbours have offered to help out, but they all have their own harvest and livestock to look after. There's no way Aunt Faye and Uncle Paul could stay over in Toronto.

Mom's arms tighten around me. "No — they decided she's stable enough to keep her in Plattsworth Hospital. Her parents being able to visit is more important right now than more specialists. And her CAT scan this morning showed that the swelling in her brain is down a bit, so they don't have to operate. With luck she'll keep improving and regain consciousness soon."

"And are you guys going to the hospital today?" I can't even look at Mom's face, I just talk into her silver-streaked hair.

"Yes, they'll let other family members in today. But only one at a time, and only for a few minutes."

"Will we all go?"

Mom loosens her hold on me so she can massage her forehead, as if she has a bad headache. "If you want to," she says. "But you don't have to."

"I won't be able to keep from crying."

Dad reaches across the table and pats my hand. "That's

okay." His voice is calm and gentle. "Cry all you want. What happened to Clare is terrible."

"Thanks." I snuggle closer to Mom. "I feel like nothing will ever be the same again."

"I know," she says, "I know." She strokes my head and rocks me like a baby. "And you're right — it won't be. Even if Clare comes through this, it will take a long time for her to fully recover." Then we're both bawling.

"Glen's camp called back," Dad says. "They'll put him on a bus, and we can pick him up this afternoon after we go to the hospital."

I make a horrible hiccupping sound. "So you must think Clare's going to die? I mean, if you're bringing Glen down here."

"No, Morgan," Dad says in his most authoritative voice. "I don't think Clare's going to die. We just wanted both of you with us right now."

"But Dad?" I sniffle. "And Mom?" I rub at my eyes and nose and then the words come out in a croaky whisper. "I'm afraid to see her."

I worried all night about that. Seeing Grandpa in hospital was scary and weird, but he was old. How can I stand to see Clare all hooked up to tubes and machines and stuff?"

"Oh, Morgan," Mom says. "Oh dear, it's so hard, I know. Maybe it's better you don't go. Because if she doesn't pull through," here she shoots Dad a look which tells me they don't agree on this, "wouldn't you rather remember her alive and beautiful?"

"No!" I shout. "No! I don't want to remember her at all. I want her to be okay. I want the accident not to have happened." And then what I remember is my own part in this. I pull away from Mom and run outside.

I hide in Seraphina's Circle all morning. I lie on the soft brown needles and close my eyes so I won't see the ruined dolls. My body feels like I'm the one in a coma. But my mind keeps whirling. I can't stop the memories of all the hours I spent here with Clare and Dulcy, hours when we pretended that Clare was Seraphina. The replays run over and over.

But it was only a game.

Clare isn't really Seraphina.

So why is she hurt?

I just don't get it. All I really know is that I'm to blame. And I'd give anything to change what I've done.

But wishing won't help. I can't make Clare okay. And I can't forget for a single minute either. So I just lie here, feeling miserable.

It seems like forever before Mom comes looking for me. She doesn't enter Seraphina's Circle, just kneels on the braided grass at the edge and asks, "So what do you think? Do you want to go over to the hospital?"

I open my eyes and sit up. "Is Dulcy going?"

"No." Mom's voice is soft through the balsam boughs. "She'll stay home to look after the Bees. We could drop you over there if you like."

I scramble out of Seraphina's Circle to Mom's side. "I guess I don't really feel like it." I fiddle with the grass, undoing one of the braids. "I think I need to be alone for awhile."

Mom frowns and puts an arm around me. "Are you sure that's a good idea? I hate to think of you here all by yourself. What will you do?"

"I'll read," I say. "I've got lots of books. I just started a good one yesterday."

"Well okay then, if you're sure." Mom rubs my back a bit. "But Morgan? There's something else. We need to talk about Saturday."

I start braiding the grass again. "What's to talk about?" I can't go to the all-star meet. It would be so wrong. I mustn't give it another thought. I need to visualize Clare getting better, not me jumping over a stupid pole.

Mom takes a deep breath, then exhales with a whooshing sound. "I know you probably don't feel like it right now," she says, "but I think you should still go. Clare would want you to."

"I can't!" I throw myself into Mom's arms and sob against her shoulder. "I just can't," I say when I've settled down. "Not if Clare's still in hospital."

"Hey, hey," Mom whispers. "It's okay, Morgan. It's okay. Let's talk about it later."

I shake my head. It isn't okay. Mom doesn't understand. Even if Clare wakes up by Saturday, there's no point in me going to the all-star meet. I made Clare have an accident. She isn't going to have a miraculous recovery. Her life is changed — it will never be the same again. And neither will mine.

My confidence is shattered. My focus is lost.

When the grownups have left for the hospital, I bring my book out to Seraphina's Circle. I try to read, but I can't concentrate. I turn the pages, but I can't even remember the character's name. I just keep thinking about Clare. Fantasy worlds? I wish. But right now I have to live in the real world, in real time. And here my only fantasy is that Clare's accident never happened.

13

IT'S LATE EVENING WHEN MY PARENTS AND GRANDMA ARRIVE back at the farm with Glen. After my wretched afternoon I'm desperate to talk. "So, how's camp?" I ask my little brother. He looks good — both taller and thinner than I remember.

Glen grins, the first smile I've seen all day. "Great!" Then he looks upset. "At least, it was, until, uh, you know."

"Yeah, I know."

"Look, I went on a nine-day canoe trip," Glen says, spreading some photos on the table. "It rained the last three days and we were soaked. But it was awesome!"

"Cool," I say. "I didn't even know you could paddle."

"I got my advanced level before we went," Glen says. "And I passed some swimming levels too." As he talks on about camp and shows me photos of his friends and counsellors, I realize we're having a conversation, not a fight.

Maybe Mom was right about sending Glen away. He does seem more mature. Too bad her plan for me didn't work out so well. Because I haven't become more like Clare at all — I just helped her get hurt.

When there's nothing left to do but go to bed, I head upstairs. I lie awake for hours. Exhausted but unable to sleep, I listen to crickets chirping somewhere out in the darkness. Voices drift up from the verandah below my window, mixed with the steady creaking of Grandma's rocking chair. It's three in the morning. Nobody else can sleep either.

"God must have had a reason for Clare's accident," Grandma says.

"If he did, it's darn hard to think what it could have been," Dad answers.

"Don't be bitter, Jim," Grandma says. "Be thankful she's got a fighting chance."

"A fighting chance at what? You heard what Faye told us. If … or when Clare wakes up, she may well have permanent physical and mental disabilities."

"That girl is a blessing," Grandma says, "such a blessing. No matter what her prognosis."

So what Dulcy told me is true. Clare might not ever be the same again.

I can't accept that. I just can't.

And then it hits me — what about Clare? How's she supposed to accept it?

And then I'm so ashamed of what a self-centred suck I've been. I really thought missing the summer in Northington was such a big deal. But it's nothing. Nothing at all compared to what Clare is missing — or maybe will be.

I thought winning at high jump was the most important thing in the world. Now I see that beating Arden wouldn't prove anything. It wouldn't matter at all.

"Oh, poor Faye," I hear Mom moan. "Poor Paul and the kids. I just ache for them."

I didn't think I could feel any more guilty, but I do now. I've been so caught up in my own mess I haven't thought about anybody else at all. I should have gone to the hospital today, or at least gone over to be with Dulcy.

Why does caring so much make showing I care so hard?

Is Dulcy lying awake too, I wonder? Alone in the room she shares with Clare, the bed beside her empty? Does she hate me? Does she wish it was me that was in hospital?

Probably everybody does.

*

Everyone sleeps in the next day. There's no reason at all to get up early. In the afternoon the grownups drive to Plattsworth to visit Clare again. "You guys want to come along?" Mom asks.

"Nah, I'll walk over to the Laing farm and hang out with the Bees," Glen says. "I want to show them my photos of camp, and maybe we can play ball or something."

"Good idea," Dad says. "Then Dulcy can come with us. Morgan?"

"Um, I guess I'll just stay here."

"You sure?" Mom sounds disappointed.

"Yeah. Didn't sleep last night — I'm too tired to go." Some excuse. But how can I say I'm still too chicken to see Clare in hospital? Especially if Dulcy's there. I don't know how I'll ever face Dulcy again. I won't know what to say or how to act — I'll just cry. I'm so ashamed of walking around alive and well while Clare can't.

The day folds over me like a thick blanket I can't kick free of. For a while I slump in front of the TV, not really watching. I think about phoning Jade and leaving her a message — I'm pretty sure she'd call back if I told her about Clare. But I can't find the energy. Each minute feels as long as an hour. Each hour is full of this awful emptiness. And I know what I'm feeling isn't even half as bad as what it will be like for Clare when she comes to.

Finally I slouch out to Seraphina's Circle. I need to *do* something. Anything. And when I see the ruined dolls I know what that thing is. I gather all the husks into a pile, every last shred. I pull up the bottom of my T-shirt to make a kind of pocket for them. And then I dump them all in the ditch.

Now what?

Back inside Seraphina's Circle, I scowl at the pine cone house Dulcy built for her Clare and Renzo dolls. I want to kick it apart. But I stop myself just in time. I know that might feel great right now, but I'd be sorry later. And anyway, I've already hurt Dulcy enough by wrecking the dolls. By not being with her the last two days. By not even phoning her.

I am such a *horrible* person.

I made Clare have an accident.

And then I let Dulcy down.

I can't stay in Seraphina's Circle. I have no right to such a special place. And anyway, with Clare in hospital, the magic is lost forever. The game we played about Seraphina seems so far in the past. And it seems weird — both too real and totally make-believe. I don't know — after wanting so much to grow up, now I wish I could be a little kid again.

I crawl out over the braided grass and wander about in the yard. What am I going to do all day? Then I see my high-jump standards and pole leaning against the side of the farmhouse.

Although I promised myself I wouldn't, I can't help thinking about the all-star meet again. I won't be there. But Arden will. Everything is ruined.

I'll never jump again.

I don't deserve to.

I grab the bamboo pole, and this time I can't help myself. I try to break it over my knee. It won't give. But I don't stop. I prop the pole against the house and stomp on it, harder and harder and harder. I keep on going until it finally snaps.

14

WAKING UP IS THE WORST. FOR THE FIRST FEW SECONDS, as the sun brightens the day and I open my eyes, I don't remember about Clare. Then wham! The details of her accident hit me all over again. And I have to face this reality: Clare is lying comatose in the hospital while I'm waking up healthy in Mom's old bedroom.

How fair is that?

So I decide to go see Clare. No more lame excuses. Visiting the hospital can't be worse than hanging around the farm all day doing nothing but hating myself.

Getting dressed I feel like I'm trapped in a bad dream. I wish I could be back in June, back before I came to the farm, back when high jump and Jade and Jeff Tan were all that mattered.

Back when Clare was okay.

I pull on the sundress Mom wants me to wear. I don't like it, but Mom is so upset I guess it's the least I can do for her. Too bad the dress doesn't suit me. Blossom pink cotton, with a long ruffly skirt, it's something Clare might wear. Which is exactly what Mom had in mind when she bought it. Except that Clare would look romantic and elegant, not childish.

Plus this dorky dress reminds me of the day last spring

when I tried to be friends with Arden. When she came over after school, Arden searched my closet to see what she might like to borrow. Nothing, of course. She prefers more revealing stuff like Lycra micro-minis and bare-midriff tops. So my dress cracked her right up. She called it a flower girl's dress and said it would look cute on a seven-year-old.

I won't look in the mirror. The dress is bad enough, but I can't stand the sight of my own face. If only I'd told Grandma what was going on with Clare and Renzo. If only I hadn't agreed to take Renzo's calls. If only I hadn't given Clare his message. If only, if only, if only. The words whirl around in my head and then settle there like the dust over Grandma's cornfield, making a thick grey layer of grief.

Downstairs, Glen snorts with laughter when he sees me.

What a brat! How dare he laugh when I've finally got my nerve up to go to the hospital? "Little creep," I say, messing up his hair.

Glen dances around me, pretending to box. "*Not* pretty in pink! *Not* pretty in pink!"

"I was wrong yesterday — you haven't changed at all." I grab at his shirt to stop him. When I get a good hold, I jab him in the stomach. "Big blubber baby!"

"Fight!" Glen yells. "Chick attack!"

Our parents come running. Dad grabs me and pins back my arms. "Hey! Cut it out." He must have been shaving, and his face is still half-covered with foam. "What do you think you're doing?"

"He started it!" I shriek, struggling to get free.

Dad looks at Glen, who's acting all innocent now. "I don't think so," he says. "And anyway, you're the oldest. You should know better."

Dad lets me go and just as he walks away, Glen whispers, "Suck it up, sis!"

I lunge at him, screaming, "I hate him! I hate him!" Dad grabs me again and Glen disappears.

Mom finishes buttoning the front of her cream linen dress. "Settle down, just settle down *please*," she begs. "Everybody's upset. Let's just keep getting ready as best we can."

"I am *not* upset!" I break away from Dad and run back to my room. "I just hate Glen! I wish it was *him* that got hurt!" I slam the door and throw myself on the bed.

In a few minutes someone knocks. I don't answer. I don't need the get-a-grip parental lecture.

But it's Grandma, and she comes in anyway. "Morgan, sweetheart," she says, "we know you didn't mean that."

"Did so!" I stare at the daisies and rosebuds of the wallpaper.

"You're just worried about going to the hospital." Grandma rests on the edge of the bed beside me. "We all understand that."

Maybe I made a mistake. Maybe I'm not ready to see Clare. Maybe I can't do this after all. "Oh Gram," I sob into my pillow. "Why did it happen? *Why?*"

"I wish I could tell you," Grandma says, rubbing my back a bit. "But I can't. I just don't know."

The name Seraphina hangs in the air between us. I shudder. I think of how Clare and Dulcy and I loved to act out Seraphina's story as if her life were a game. Just a bit of make-believe. But did our pretending somehow make this happen to Clare?

"Sometimes life is very difficult." Grandma massages my shoulders and kneads my backbone. "This is one of those times."

I just lie there, silent.

"Oh, Morgan. I know that sounds simplistic."

"Yes."

"Well, look at it this way. You know about high jump, don't you?"

I turn over and sit up. "What about it?"

"Well, as you get better, you keep trying to jump higher, to challenge yourself."

"So?"

"And the more you ask of yourself, the more difficult it is."

"I still don't get what you mean."

"What I mean is, a height you haven't jumped before is difficult. You might have to try a few times, maybe a lot of times, before you can clear it. Well, life is full of things like that. Like Clare's accident. You come up against them, and you just have to find a way to get over."

"And then what?"

"And then you get on with the rest of your life."

"But Gram, what if you never make that jump? What if there's something you can never, ever, get over? Something impossible to clear?"

"I was afraid you'd ask me that." Grandma unbuttons the jacket of her fuchsia suit, which looks much too hot for a summer day. I'm not sure if she and Mom think that dressing up to go to the hospital will somehow help Clare, or if it just makes them feel better. "Some people reach a point in their lives that stops them cold. They can't get over and they can't go on. And they start to wither away inside."

She studies the hem of my dress, running the ruffled edge between her fingers. "That's what happened to your great-grandfather Hamish. After Seraphina died, his heart shrivelled into a hopeless, wretched knot. And it almost happened to me. I blamed myself for a long, long time. But when I finally married I made a conscious decision to forget the past and live in the present."

"I'm not sure I can do that." Because how can I ever forgive myself?

Grandma smoothes my hair back off my forehead. "Listen Morgan," she says. "You have to accept Clare's accident and what it means so you can be a good friend to her. You will always be sad somewhere inside about this. But sadness is as much a part of life as happiness. You *will* learn to live with it. And you'll be a better, stronger person for it."

"Oh."

"The doctors say Clare's young enough that there's hope she can mostly recover in time. But she's going to need all our strength and support to do that." Grandma hugs me, hard, and stands up. "And now I really need to finish getting ready. You should, too."

I watch Grandma straighten her skirt and tug at her jacket as she walks away. I wish she could stay and hold me a bit longer. "Okay," I say. "I'll try."

But what if Grandma's wrong? After all, she doesn't know that I gave Clare Renzo's message. She doesn't know that's what made Clare hurry. And she doesn't know that Clare, who was always so careful, crashed the tractor into the ditch because she was in a rush to meet Renzo.

It's not time to leave for the hospital yet, but I can't stay inside. I can't face Seraphina's Circle either. So I wander out into the cornfield where Dulcy and I walked my first day at the farm. The day Dulcy found the bit of buckle.

The corn, almost full-grown now, stands taller than me. The stalks look like silky-haired ladies in long green dresses. In my ruffly pink cotton I feel as out of place as the ragweed and clover crowding in between the rows.

But it's peaceful in the cornfield. A light breeze rustles the stalks while butterflies flit about and meadowlarks sing. Maybe I can skip the hospital. Maybe I can hide here forever. Cornfields are good hiding places. The deeper I push into the rows the harder it is to walk. The elegant green leaves aren't as gentle as they look. When I part them so I can pass, they scratch my arms with a sharp, hairy stickiness.

And then I feel someone following me. Glen.

"Hey, little brother, you could get lost out here."

"Not a chance."

"Like, duh? You know the way back?" Out in the middle of the cornfield, everything looks the same. There is no beginning or end. Just acres and acres of corn. "If I were to leave you alone, no one would ever find you," I say. "Alive, that is. Bet nobody knows you're out here."

Glen stamps the soil, making a puff of dust rise around me.

"Oh, and don't look up either. You might get smut in your eyes, and then you'd be blind too."

Of course he looks up right away. A greyish-black blob hangs at the top of some of the cobs. Grandma says it's a kind of fungus.

"That?" Glen asks, pointing.

"Don't look!" I yell. "It's diseased. It's mutant. And now you are too!" I turn and dash away, the corn leaves scraping at my arms and legs. I know I'm being mean, but life is mean sometimes, isn't that what Grandma was just telling me? So why shouldn't I be mean too?

"Wait, Morgan, wait!"

"Stupid corn mutant! You can't run fast enough to follow me!"

But Glen can. He catches up. And then at the end of the cornrow he sprints right past me. He must have been training at camp or something.

As I burst out of the field behind him, I see our parents and Grandma just stepping into the car. Mom is glancing around, a concerned look on her face.

"For heaven's sake, Morgan!" she calls when she sees me. "You look a wreck! What on earth were you doing?"

"Sorry, Mom." I stare down at the silly sandals I'm wearing. My feet are dusty from the cornfield, but not dusty enough to hide their sickly white colour. After wearing runners all summer, my feet are totally untanned. They look like dead bodies stuck on the ends of my legs. "Glen got lost and I had to rescue him." It's scary how good I'm getting at lying. I almost believe that one myself.

"Well, get in the car now. You'll have to fix your hair on the way."

Nobody talks at all as we bump along over the rough washboard road. Tugging at my frizzy hair with Mom's brush, I pull harder than I need to. I want it to hurt. After all, Clare is hurt. And I'm a mean liar. Pull, yank, hurt. Then with my scalp stinging I glare out the window. Bulrushes fill the ditches lining the dusty roadside, waving in the wind, rippling on and on for miles.

All the way to the hospital.

15

PLATTSWORTH REGIONAL HOSPITAL LOOMS AT THE TOP OF the main street of town. As we drive towards it, I see the people who live here going about their business, having an ordinary day. They're doing their banking and shopping and meeting for coffee. But we're going to the hospital to visit Clare.

Mom takes my arm as we enter the lobby. It feels both scary and comforting here, like sadness and hope are all mixed up together. As we head down the hall a smell of cleaning products and bodily functions hangs in the air.

Clare's room is right beside the nurses' station, but the door is closed. While Mom checks for updates on Clare's condition, I go on down the hall to the visitors' lounge. Looking in through the windows I see Aunt Faye sitting in a chair, her head in her hands. Did she sleep here again? I know she did the first couple of nights, in case Clare woke up.

I go back to Mom. "Oh, but that's wonderful," I hear her saying to the nurse at the desk. "Clare opened her eyes this morning," she tells us, "just briefly, and she didn't really come to, but that's such a good sign."

Then Grandma and Dad and Glen go into the lounge and Mom leads me into Clare's room. "Now remember what we talked about, how she's going to look," Mom says, pushing me forward but keeping a tight hold on my arm.

Yeah, we talked about this, but I'm still not prepared for the sight of my beautiful cousin lying there in a coma hooked up to tubes and stuff.

The nurse follows us in and busies herself with changing the bags of fluid hanging on the IV pole and then the catheter bag. Clare can't even pee by herself. The nurse checks the dressings on Clare's legs and then smoothes the pastel-blue blankets back in place. Clare's gown is blue too, with a pattern of little white clouds. Her hair is greasy and tied back off her face, which looks all stiff and waxy. Her closed eyes look puffy and bruised.

"Her legs are healing nicely," the nurse tells us. "The doctors are really pleased. And you know she opened her eyes for a few seconds this morning." She takes Clare's temperature and blood pressure, pushes back her eyelids and shines a light in her pupils, then makes some notes on a chart clipped to the end of Clare's bed. "You can talk to her," she says to me. "She's not in a deep coma — she does have some responses. So tell her stuff, anything at all. She might just know you're here."

Anything at all? She's kidding — right? Because what can you say to a beautiful teenage girl who's lying there hooked up to scary hospital equipment and looking dead? There is only one word. *Sorry.* And as Mom's often told me, sometimes sorry's not enough.

Mom gives me a pat on the back and leaves me alone with Clare. I'm sweating and shaking. All I want to do is run away. But the mound of Clare's crushed legs under the blanket stops me. She had multiple fractures. Now her legs are held together with steel rods and pins and skin grafts and stitches. Even when she has physio and relearns to walk, she's going to have severe scarring. And then there will be more operations when she's fully grown.

Sorry's not enough, but I have to try. I make myself take her hand, the one without the IV needle. It's cool and limp in mine. There are white bands on her fingers from where she wears her silver rings. Her only jewellery today is a plastic hospital wrist band.

I lean over and whisper in her ear. "Clare? It's me, Morgan. I love you and I am so, so sorry." I wait, but she doesn't wake up. She doesn't do anything at all but breathe. I squeeze her hand and say, "Can you hear me, Clare? Please, please, if you can, squeeze back."

Nothing.

"Hey Clare," I say. "Want a laugh? Wake up and see me in a girly pink dress." I squeeze her hand some more. "Hey, you got a whole lot of chocolates and flowers here, you know? You should see them — it's like a Laura Secord store. There's even a dozen red roses from Renzo. So open your eyes, okay? C'mon Clare, wake up or I'll eat all your candy." Squeeze, squeeze, squeeze.

Still nothing.

Then Dad and Glen come in and I rush out. I find Mom and Grandma and Aunt Faye in the lounge, talking in excited voices. Aunt Faye is babbling about Clare opening her eyes for three seconds this morning. "Oh, my Lord, I am so glad I was there when it happened," she's saying. "I know she saw me, she almost smiled, I'm sure of it, oh, I'm so relieved, and the doctor is going to cut back on the sedatives now, because the swelling in her brain has gone down so much, and then she's likely to come to soon."

Oh yeah? I can't look at Aunt Faye — she's way too hopeful. Instead I fuss with the ruffly skirt of my pink dress that would look lovely on Clare. Then I study my tanned arms, scratched from the cornfield, and my pale, dusty, dead-body feet.

We stay all day. We visit Clare for a few minutes, one or two of us at a time, then we wait in the lounge. For variety we walk up and down the hall, buy snacks from the vending machines, or go sit in the cafeteria.

Coming back from having lunch, Glen and I see Renzo in the lobby, just leaving the hospital. He's with Clare's best friend Nicole. Nicole works in Plattsworth, but Renzo must have driven all the way over here on his lunch hour. "Hey, Renzo!" I call. "Nicole!"

Renzo looks right through me and keeps on going out the revolving door. But Nicole stops, and we hug each other. She bursts into tears. After she stops crying we talk a little about Clare's accident.

"Ohmigod," Nicole says, over and over. "I can't believe what happened. Clare's so nice — she didn't deserve that."

"How's Renzo doing?"

"He's really upset, but he won't talk about it. And believe me, I've tried."

She's tried? Like, she's *been there* for him? "Guys, eh?" I say. "They hate to talk about emotional stuff." Not that I know this, but it's what Jade says.

"I wrote a poem for Clare?" Nicole says. "But I didn't read it to her. I was waiting till she woke up, but she didn't, so I put it in the drawer beside her bed?" We see Renzo's car pull up, and she waves to show him she'll only be a minute. "If she wakes up when you're here, can you read it to her for me?

I gotta go now, but I'll try to come again soon."

"Sure." I watch as she climbs into Renzo's car and they drive away. Hmm. I wonder if they'll start going out together? It'll be ages before Clare can go out again.

If she *ever* can.

And will Renzo still love Clare if she's not the same?

Back in the lounge, there's a family with a crying baby and three little kids watching cartoons. Glen joins them, but I go into the chapel area at the other end where Mom, Dad, Grandma and Aunt Faye are sitting. It's the quietest place in the hospital, away from everything. I sit beside Dad, who is pretending to read a magazine. But really he's sitting there with the pages open in front of his face to hide the tears trickling down his cheeks.

I've never seen my Dad cry before. I didn't think he could. I mean, I thought he was too old or something. Mom says when Dad was a kid boys didn't cry, so now he doesn't know how. Maybe I should hand him a tissue? But I get the feeling he'd rather be left alone. Being a guy and all.

What's really weird is that I'm *not* crying. After so many tears the past few days, I didn't even cry with Nicole. It seems I'm the only dry-eyed person here today.

Stained-glass windows frame both sides of the chapel. A brass plaque on the wall explains how these windows were donated by families whose relatives died in Plattsworth Regional Hospital, in memory of their loved ones. Great. Like, that's *so* reassuring.

Sunlight streaming through the windows casts funny coloured patterns on my dress. I look around and notice red diamonds on Aunt Faye's neck and blue squares on Grandma's shoulder.

A streak of green light cuts across one side of Mom's face, jutting up and over her head. She looks totally ridiculous. I have a wicked urge to laugh.

Mom turns to keep the sun out of her eyes. But that exposes her cheek and ear even more to the weird green light, which flashes off her gold clip-on earrings. Mom only wears earrings for what she calls *good*. But what's *good* about this?

I bite my tongue and pinch myself. But it doesn't work. I start to giggle anyway.

And then I can't stop. A high, cackling noise sputters out of me like fireworks. I bend my head, my face in my hands, trying to sound like I'm crying.

But there's no doubt about it. I'm laughing. Laughing my stupid head off, right in the middle of the hospital chapel. How bizarre is that? What is *wrong* with me? And why can't I stop?

Then Grandma comes and takes me by the hand, saying she needs to go to the washroom and maybe I should come with her. When we get there I'm finally able to control myself. I take a tissue from Grandma and blow my nose, and we both pretend I've been crying really hard.

Back in the chapel, Aunt Faye gives me a funny look. But I can't tell if it's stern and angry, or just plain sad. Please, please, please, don't let her know I was laughing. I'd never be able to explain. I have no idea why it happened — only that it shouldn't have. I can't believe what a nasty person I am. Except for my part in Clare's accident, it's the worst thing I've ever done.

16

AFTER OUR LONG DAY AT THE HOSPITAL VISITING CLARE, it's early evening before we get back to Grandma's. Aunt Faye wanted to go home tonight to get some sleep, so Mom invited her and Uncle Paul, Dulcy and the Bees over to eat dinner with us. They've brought a lot of food with them — food that neighbours dropped off at the Laing farm to help the family cope. Aunt Faye told us earlier that the inside of their fridge is so full it looks like the day before the annual picnic.

But I snacked so much today that I don't feel like eating. All I want is a shower. In the car all of our clothes and even our hair smelled like the hospital. I hurry past Dulcy saying, "Gotta get changed."

In the bathroom I strip off my pink dress as fast as I can, then borrow Grandma's jasmine-rose shower gel to scrub myself down with. I use her vanilla shampoo to wash my hair. When I pull on my jean shorts and a clean T-shirt I feel so much better. The shirt smells especially fresh, since Grandma hangs our laundry out on the line to dry.

And then I hide upstairs.

I *so* don't want to talk to Dulcy. How can I tell her that we visited all day and that Clare only opened her eyes for a few seconds before we got there? Or that I saw Renzo with

Nicole? And what if Aunt Faye tells Dulcy about me laughing in the chapel?

I wish I'd stayed at the hospital and slept in Clare's room. I'd hate for her to wake up and find nobody there. Sure, the nurses are watching most of the time, but still. Clare wouldn't know where she was, or what's happened.

She'll be all alone and scared.

I can't go back to the hospital to help Clare tonight. But maybe I should go find Dulcy. Maybe I can help her instead. She's been home by herself with the Bees all day — Uncle Paul would have been busy with farm work. I'm sure she feels alone and scared too.

Dulcy's not in the house, so I look around outside. Of course she's in Seraphina's Circle. She's sitting by her dolls' pine cone house, arms hugging her knees, sobbing. But though the sight of her breaks my heart, I don't know what to do. Somehow it just feels too hard to go up to her. In the end I decide not to disturb her. I tell myself I'll come back later.

I don't want to go back inside though, so I head around behind the barn. But Aunt Faye is out there, perched on the barnyard gate, staring at the wall where I lobbed the eggs.

I backtrack quickly and hide in Grandma's garden. Crouched low in the masses of mauve phlox, I let them comfort me. These flowers come up every year and bloom without anyone tending them. They self-seed and keep going, no matter what's happening with the people who live here.

In a few minutes I feel someone touch my shoulder. "Hi," Aunt Faye says. "Mind if I join you?"

I burst into tears. "I'm sorry," I sob. "I wish it could have been me that got hurt instead of Clare. And I know everybody else does, too."

Aunt Faye drops down beside me, holding me until I settle. "Now listen here, Morgan," she says. "Nothing can change what happened. But nobody, *absolutely nobody*, wishes it was you instead."

"But it was all my fault!" I wail. And suddenly I'm spilling everything out to her. "Renzo phoned me to make a time for them to meet, and I gave Clare the message, and if I hadn't, she might not have hurried, and she might have been more careful, and she might not have had an accident."

Aunt Faye tugs at her long black skirt, which is all bunched up under her. "I know," she says.

"*You know?*"

"Yes." With a grim little smile Aunt Faye says, "Renzo came to talk to me at the hospital last night. He told me everything too."

"Oh."

"He thought it was all his fault, you see." Aunt Faye shakes her head. "And I'd been thinking it was all my fault, for being so strict with her, forcing them to meet in secret." She fiddles with the charm bracelet on her wrist. "I got this for my sixteenth birthday," she says, "and I was — *I am* — going to give it to Clare on her sixteenth next fall." She shows me a tiny gold baby shoe. "This is the charm your mom and dad gave me when Clare was born."

A horrible gasping sound comes out of me. Aunt Faye politely ignores it just the way she ignored — or at least hasn't mentioned — me laughing in the hospital chapel today.

"Anyway," she says, "I know Paul feels it's all *his* fault, for ever letting her drive that tractor in the first place. He knew it wasn't the safest piece of machinery on earth."

"Oh." Why didn't he fix it then? Or get rid of it? What

was he thinking?

"But of course it's not his fault. He does the best he can with five kids and a farm to run — it's not like he's ever just sitting around watching TV. And that tractor usually worked well enough." Aunt Faye's voice breaks as she speaks.

"Yeah, it did," I say. "Clare drove it just fine lots of times. I mean, she knew what it was like, how to handle it." But I still want to blame somebody.

As if she knows what I'm thinking, Aunt Faye says, "It's not *anybody's* fault. We'll all end up crazy if we think like that." She's quiet for a bit, then she continues like she's trying to convince herself, "It was an accident, and accidents happen."

"Or it could have been a punishment." My voice sounds tiny and scared.

Aunt Faye looks puzzled. "A punishment?"

"Yeah, you know, because we went behind your back and all. Clare and I knew it was wrong, sneaking around, but we did it anyway." I press my cheek against the phlox, breathing in their spicy fragrance. "Sort of like Seraphina," I say into the flowers. "Her father forbade her to see Jed, but she didn't care. She tried anyway, and she got killed."

"Oh my lord!" Aunt Faye sounds disgusted. "I knew Grandma should never have told you girls that story. She's obsessed with it — she's never gotten over her guilt."

"But it is kind of the same, isn't it?"

Now Aunt Faye bursts into tears. "No!" she cries. "It's not. Accidents happen, and then we have to live with the consequences. Sure, maybe Clare could have been more careful, or *maybe* she could have been luckier. Maybe I could have been more understanding of how she felt about Renzo, or *maybe* it could have rained that day. Our actions are only part of the way the world works. There's a whole lot of random chance out there too."

I think about that for a minute. "So you're saying that no matter how good you are, bad stuff can still happen to you, just by chance?"

"Yes," Aunt Faye says. "That's exactly what I mean."

"Okay." I touch the little gold baby shoe on Aunt Faye's bracelet. "I guess that makes me feel better. But it doesn't help Clare."

Aunt Faye takes my face in her hands and turns it so she can look me straight in the eye. "Listen to me, Morgan. Clare is alive, and someday she's going to be okay again."

I return her hopeful gaze. "Yeah, I sure hope so." And then I have to look away.

Aunt Faye pulls a tissue from her pocket and blows her nose. "I must believe that," she says. "I couldn't go on if I didn't. But you know what else? I'm glad Clare defied me. I'm glad she saw Renzo. I mean, just in case she doesn't fully recover, it's good to know she had at least one summer of being in love."

"Oh, Aunt Faye," I say. "She did. I mean, she does. She and Renzo are really in love." I remember seeing Renzo and Nicole at the hospital and wonder what will happen. But for now that's all Aunt Faye needs to know. It feels way too grown-up, but I reach for her hand. "What about you?" I ask. "How will you manage?"

"Oh, we'll get the work done one way or another. The Bees will have to help more, and if we have to, we'll hire another hand."

"That's good," I say, "but it's not what I meant. I was talking about you." I squeeze her hand the way I did Clare's.

But Aunt Faye squeezes back.

"Thanks," she says. "I guess I'll just keep busy. And I'll try to take nothing for granted from now on. You know — make every minute count, for Clare's sake." Then she pulls herself up off the ground, saying, "I'd better go see how Dulcy is."

Yeah, I was supposed to see how Dulcy was too. But I sit there in the flowers for a while longer anyway, thinking about what Aunt Faye said. When I go back to the house, the Laing family is ready to leave. And as they drive away, I see Dulcy waving at me from the back seat.

Dulcy.

I have to see her. Not tomorrow or the next day. Like, now.

Tonight.

17

I don't tell anyone where I'm going. I just start walking.

I sure hope the cattle won't be out in the field by the back lane.

But of course they are, because the Bees haven't been home yet to bring them in. They herd by the gate as if they've been waiting for me. I stop at the spot where Dulcy and I used to leave flowers for Seraphina. Maybe I should go back. Yeah. I should go back. Mom might be worried if she can't find me.

But I have to see Dulcy. I have to. This can't wait any longer.

I grit my teeth and climb over the gate. With one hand in a tight fist and the other in my pocket, I glare at the cattle as I race past. I run all the way to the Laing barnyard. There, gasping and sweating, I stop to catch my breath. And then I see Dulcy trudging towards me.

She's wearing a sundress printed with dragonflies that belongs to Clare. It's way too big and long for her, but she's got it pulled in and up at the waist with a blue ribbon sash. She looks so little. And so pathetic. I want to run away.

But it's too late. Dulcy's already seen me.

"Hi," she calls. "I was just coming over to find you."

"Really? Well, I was just coming over to find you." My right hand is still in my pocket. "I've got something for you."

"And I've got something for you." A proud smile spreads across Dulcy's face, and she hikes the dress up some more.

"What is it?"

"What have you got?"

I pull my hand out of my pocket. Then I open my fist to show her my half of Seraphina's buckle. My palm is covered with red marks from gripping it so hard as I passed the cattle. "This is for us to share, Dulcy," I say. "I'm sorry I was mean and kept it so long. It's your turn to have it now."

"Oh! But you have to take this." Dulcy holds out the other half of the buckle.

"What?" I say. "I don't understand."

"It's Clare's half," Dulcy says. "I want you to have it, so both parts can be together. It might help Clare get better."

"Oh, Dulcy," I say. "That can't work — you know that can't make her better."

"But I was looking at her things," Dulcy says, "and I saw it, and ..."

"So that's where the dress came from, huh? Clare's closet?"

"She won't mind that I wore it," Dulcy says, "will she?"

"No. She'll be happy you're wearing it. It looks great."

Dulcy wraps her ribbon sash around her free hand and gives me her buckle half. "Keep the two pieces of the buckle together, at Grandma's house," she says. "Please?"

"Okay, sure." Whatever she wants. It can't make things worse.

We hug each other, laughing and crying at the same time. And then Dulcy is sniffing at my hair. "Hey," she says, "your hair smells good."

"Thanks. I tried Grandma's shampoo." I don't ﹍ention that I had to get the hospital smell off me. "Mom doesn't like me to buy those fancy, scented products. But Gram loves them."

"I wish you were my big sister," Dulcy says into my shoulder. "You know about stuff."

"But you have Clare."

"I mean, besides Clare. Because what if she doesn't get better?"

I pull away. "Dulcy, don't talk like that. I'm not a good big sister — just ask Glen. He can't stand me."

"I don't care. I like you."

"Thanks." I fasten the two halves of the buckle together, clinking them into a whole butterfly. "Look, Dulcy. It almost goes with your dress." We try to fasten the buckle onto the ribbon belt, but it's way too heavy. We give up, and I put the buckle into my pocket. "Guess I'd better go now," I say.

Dulcy looks out at the horizon, where the sun is making the evening sky all rosy. "It'll be dark soon. Want me to walk with you?"

"No, it's okay. I made it over here, I guess I'll make it back." I watch as Dulcy heads back to her house, tripping over the hem of Clare's dress.

For the first time ever I don't feel scared passing the cattle. I'm almost tempted to herd them up and back to their barn to save the Bees the trouble. "Co bossie, co bossie," I call to them as I cross the field. I'm not sure what those words mean, but my cousins say them, and I like the way they sound. I like not being afraid too.

The light fades as I walk and the sun slips below the horizon, like a coin lost down a slot in the sky. The evening smells of fresh hay. I think about how easily I could have had an accident with that tractor if I'd ever learned to drive it. But I didn't. And I'm okay, but Clare isn't. So what does that mean?

And *is* Clare's accident somehow connected with Seraphina's?

An odd spinning feeling shivers through me, as if I'm caught in an invisible spiral. Whirled to its calm centre, I feel the air go still. So still, I feel like I can actually see how everyone is connected — not just Clare and Seraphina, everyone in the whole wide world. We're all linked to each other, and also linked to something beyond us. I feel like everything somehow makes sense.

But then, just as suddenly, the moment is gone.

*

The dishwasher is humming as I enter the kitchen. The counters are wiped, and Mom is sweeping the floor, looking exhausted. "So there you are," she says. "We were wondering."

I glance at Grandma, slumped in a chair, her feet propped up on a stool. "Sorry, Mom. Sorry, Gram. I should have stayed to help. But I needed to see Dulcy."

"That's fine, love," Grandma says. "The cleanup could have waited till tomorrow, but we needed something to do." She fans herself with a newspaper. "But I'm sure beat now. Let's have some of that iced tea Fergus brought."

"I'll get it." I hurry to the fridge. "Where's Dad and Glen?" I chunk ice into three tall glasses. "Should I pour some for them?"

Mom's eyebrows lift in surprise. "They've gone to bed already. It was a long day."

"Yeah, it sure was." I cut a lemon and place a slice over the rim of each glass.

Mom stops sweeping and sits at the table beside me. "Morgan, are you okay?"

I shrug. "No," I say. "And I won't be, as long as Clare's in the hospital, and probably for ages after that. But Aunt Faye said we should make every minute count, for Clare's sake." I sip at my tea and some dribbles down my chin.

"Oh Morgan," Mom says, reaching for me.

I sort of wipe my chin on Mom's dress as we hug. "I have to tell you something." I gulp in air and then the words come gushing out. "I told Aunt Faye, but you and Gram should know too. It was partly my fault, about Clare, because I helped her see Renzo. He phoned here to set up a time to meet her, and I pretended he was Jeff Tan, and then Clare rushed driving the tractor, so she could meet him on time and it was just like Seraphina and Jed and — "

"Hush now," Grandma says. "We know. Faye phoned while you were out. She wanted to make sure you weren't blaming yourself."

"She did?"

"She did," Mom says. "And I'm not mad at you and neither is Aunt Faye. What you did was wrong, but under the circumstances, it's understandable." She flashes Grandma a look of total frustration. "Some people just don't know when to keep quiet. I hope we've heard the end of Seraphina."

"Not to change the subject, but what about that track meet?" Grandma says. "Everyone thinks you should still go. Even Faye, she said be sure to tell you that Clare would want you to."

"I can't." I say. "I wouldn't feel right. It's too soon."

"It would do you good." Mom finishes her sweeping, empties the dustpan and puts the broom away. "Remember what you said about making every minute count? We'll drive to Northington tomorrow, then we'll bring you and Dulcy back Saturday night. Sunday we'll take Glen back to camp."

Hmm. I picture Arden thinking I won't be at the all-star meet. Thinking she has no competition. Thinking she'll win for sure. And then I picture our relay team short one runner. I'd hate to let the team down. "But I haven't practised since Monday," I say.

"You've been training all summer," Grandma reminds me. "You're ready."

They both look at me, beaming positive, *you-can-do-it* energy. I feel so much love all around me. "Yes," I say. "Yes, I am."

18

By the morning of the all-star meet, everything feels wrong again. I think of Clare and I have no energy. No confidence. No focus.

I'm not ready to jump. My head feels all fuzzy and dazed. I can barely remember the drive home to Northington or much about Jade dropping in last night. Maybe that's because she didn't stay, just came by on her way to a party. And she spent most of the time with her cell phone, checking her messages.

Only one thing is clear — Clare is still in hospital and we don't know if she's going to get better.

Am I making a huge mistake? Because I'm not sure about this. And it would be better not to compete today than to go and mess up.

I get dressed quietly, so I won't wake Dulcy in her sleeping bag on the floor. She went to bed the same time I did, but I don't think she slept at all. She was pretty excited about being here and going to the track meet today. And I know she's worried about Clare. We both are.

I pull on my Tecumseh Elementary School tank, red with white lettering. Then my red track shorts with the white stripes down the side. And then my amazing jumping shoes.

I try to slip Seraphina's belt buckle into the pocket of my shorts. But it won't fit — these shorts just have a little inside pocket for a key or a coin. Too bad. Dulcy wanted me to carry the buckle today. She thinks it will bring good luck. But even if it did fit in my pocket, it would weigh me down. It would bump against me or dig into me and distract me.

As I try to un-jam the buckle from the little mesh pocket I remember Aunt Faye's words: *Make every minute count, for Clare's sake.* And then it hits me. How can I *not* try today, when I have legs that can still jump? I *have* to go for it.

I hold the buckle in my hands and concentrate hard, seeing the pole set at 1.35, then 1.4, then 1.45. Seeing myself leap over.

When Dulcy wakes up I give her the buckle. "Here," I say. "This won't fit in my pocket, and I'd really like it if you'd hold it for me today."

"Really?" Dulcy looks like I've just told her Clare's made a complete recovery. "Thanks!" She takes the buckle in both hands and presses it against her chest. "And this time I won't lose it," she says. "I'll be right there with it when you're jumping."

It's a fine August day, sunny and hot. After breakfast, Mom drops Dulcy and Jade and me off at Northington High, where the meet is getting started.

Jade's wearing a short, pleated denim skirt with a neon orange tank top. Over the summer she's had her hair high-lighted and cut blunt with straight bangs. "I can't believe it," she says when we get out of the car. "Your mother came and picked me up, and she actually talked to me."

"I know," I say. "It's because of my cousin — Dulcy's big sister — the one that's in hospital. But let's not talk about that or I'll get all stressed out."

"Right," Jade says. "Oh wow! Look over there — who's

that guy?"

"No idea. And I've gotta go check the schedule. C'mon, Dulcy."

"Okay, catch ya later." Jade heads off towards the guy, making a call as she goes.

My skin prickles with anticipation. I love everything about meets: the chaos of kids and parents with their coolers and backpacks and mascots, the sound of the announcer's voice booming over the field, the officials with their tape measures and clipboards.

After I've found out the times of my events at the official's table, I go sit under a tree and dab sunscreen on my nose and neck. Then I hand the sunscreen to Dulcy and start stretching.

"So where's this Arden?" Dulcy asks when I'm done.

"Haven't seen her yet. But we're both on the relay team, and it's time to go find them." I lead Dulcy around the track, searching for my teammates among the groups gathered on the hillside.

Finally I see Maheesa and Roz under a big sun umbrella. "Hey!" Maheesa calls. "Sit here, my Mom's got everything set up." She points to a cooler. "Help yourself. We've got water and juice and pop."

Maheesa's being nice to me? "Thanks. Maybe later." I remember how she didn't speak to me the last two months of school. What's going on? Why's she being so friendly now? "I have to keep moving, so I won't get nervous."

"She's over there," Maheesa says, tilting her head. Off to the side, her long blonde hair tied back tightly, Arden sits alone, stretching. "We had a big fight, and I'm never speaking to her again." Maheesa's smile tells me she wants to make up.

I give her a look that says: *I'll think about it.*

When Arden sees me, she stops mid-stretch and her mouth drops open.

Jade reappears at my side and says, "I told her at the pool one day you weren't coming. Just to psych her out. Look how pissed off she is."

"Might as well take advantage of that," I say as I smile and wave over at Arden. Too bad I'll have to work with her in the qualifying relay heat, which is being called right now. Well, I can force myself to be nice for a few minutes, but can she?

Tecumseh draws the outside lane. "Okay, you guys, let's do it!" I shout as the girls gather on the track. "We can win this, no problem." I smile at Arden again. "And I'm going to beat *you* at high jump," I say under my breath. Arden flashes me a dirty look.

Roz is our first runner and she goes like crazy. I run second and keep her lead. But as I pass the baton to Maheesa, she stumbles as she takes off. She's behind when she passes the baton to Arden, our anchor. Rushing to make up the time, Arden dashes away before she has a good hold and drops the baton. She picks it up fast, but not fast enough.

We don't even make the final.

"You stupid loser!" Arden yells at Maheesa. "Why didn't you run faster?"

"You're the one that screwed up — you fumbled the baton!" Maheesa yells right back.

"Hey, it's nobody's fault," I say as I walk away from the track. "Just forget it, okay?" I can't let the lost relay ruin my day.

I'd like to hang out with Maheesa for a while and find out what happened with her and Arden. But it still hurts how she treated me. And I need to stay focused now.

There's over an hour to wait for high jump, so Jade takes off on her own again. Dulcy and I watch other events. I laugh a lot — because I'm so nervous and also because I haven't laughed in a while. It feels good. And it feels right to be here.

At last, at eleven o'clock, I hear the announcement. "First call for Midget girls' high jump, pit number two."

As I wait at the pit for practice time, my legs feel like balloons or something, fat and blobby and useless. And my mind insists on showing me scenes I don't need right now: Clare sitting with Renzo on the riverbank, Clare holding Seraphina's hair, Clare lying hooked up to tubes in the hospital.

I inhale deeply, then exhale slowly, trying to control my breathing and my thoughts. I have to shake off this slack, floaty feeling.

After final call, the official arrives and explains the rules to the twelve of us forming an eager circle around the high-jump pit. "You will each have three attempts and three run-ups, which will be considered practice if you don't leave the ground. A fourth run-up with no jump is considered a missed attempt. We'll start at 1.2 and you will each have one official practice."

I close my eyes and try to block everything but jumping.

As we work through the elimination rounds, I'm more in charge with each jump. I don't talk to anyone and I don't check out the spectators. I forbade my parents to come watch, but I have a feeling they're somewhere nearby anyway. And I know Jade and Dulcy are standing just off to the side of the pit. Dulcy held up the buckle for me to see when I walked by, and I can hear them calling to me.

"You can do it Morgan!"

"C'mon girl!"

"You know you can!"

But I can't be distracted by anyone or anything. *Focus, focus, focus,* I tell myself, *that's what you have to do.*

Jumper after jumper is eliminated, until we reach 1.4 and then there are only two of us left. Arden and me. Just like we both knew it would be.

The sun glares down. Sweat coats my whole body. I sip from my water bottle, then sprinkle a few cooling drops on my wrists and forehead.

Because I jump from the left, I can look straight across the pit at Arden. Her eyes are all red and puffy, like she's been crying. Probably she feels bad for dropping the baton in relay. Who wouldn't? Her mouth draws a straight, hard line across her face as she prepares to jump 1.42.

When she misses, I almost feel sorry for her. Almost. But not quite. Not after what she put me through. But I'm not going there now. I'm going over that pole.

I miss on my first try.

On her second attempt, Arden makes it.

I block Arden and Clare and everything else from my mind. There is nothing in the world but me and that pole. On my second try I make it too.

The official raises the pole to 1.45.

Arden misses.

I miss.

Arden misses again.

I miss again.

So this is it. One more chance.

"Arden Hampton-Price, final attempt," the official calls.

Arden keeps her eyes on the pole for several minutes before she's ready. But when she finally does run — something — I can't tell what, breaks her stride. Her takeoff is all wrong.

She doesn't even come close to making the jump. Instead of her usual bouncing backflip through the air, she just crashes right into the pole. Exactly what I made my little cornhusk doll do. Then Arden collapses on the ground, holding one ankle and yelping like a drama queen.

A sympathetic groan rises from the crowd, and the first aid crew comes running. What a faker! Arden's probably not hurt — she just wants me to mess up like she did.

As the paramedics examine her, I force myself to hold on to my focus. Even if Arden really *is* injured, I *will not* let her distract me. And if it's not fake, at least it's nothing serious — not like Clare's legs. So I can't let it intimidate me. Just like I can't worry or feel guilty about Clare right now.

I concentrate hard on my last jump.

The air around me feels charged, as if some kind of electric current is surging through it. Everything seems very bright and clear. The official calls, "Morgan Brentwood, final attempt."

"Arch your back," I hear Jade yell. "Lift your feet, watch your butt."

"Go Morgan!" Dulcy shouts. "Do it for Clare!"

Now, I command myself. Do it now.

I run.

I jump.

I fly!

My body lifts up and over.

Lying on the mat looking back at the bar, I dare it to fall

on me. But it doesn't even jiggle. When I stand the crowd cheers.

Jade appears with Dulcy at her side. "Awesome jump!" she says. "You rule!" And then she whispers, "Look behind you."

When I whirl around I'm face to face with Jeff Tan.

"Hey, you're back," he says, as if he actually cares.

I just stand there gawking at him. His straight black hair falls over his forehead in a way that makes my legs feel all wobbly again. I wait for him to say something, but he doesn't. *Ask him how's your summer going or something*, I tell myself, but what comes out is, "Are you going to Parker Pool later?"

Jeff sticks his hands in his pockets and scrubs at the ground with one foot. "Maybe," he finally says.

"Morgan!" A familiar voice calls. "That was fantastic!" As Dad folds me into a hug, Jeff Tan heads off to where Arden is walking away through the crowd. She's not even limping.

Then Mom is there with me too, laughing. But also crying. When she gets herself under control, she says, "Let's go out for lunch. To celebrate. Jade, would you like to come along?"

Jade folds up her cell phone and says, "Thanks, but I'm going to meet some friends up at the mall. I'd love a ride though."

After we drop Jade off, we go to Pastapizza, my favourite restaurant. I order a large root beer, garlic bread *and* a personal pizza with double cheese and mushrooms, and then a brownie sundae. So does Dulcy. Mom doesn't say a word about junk food or how much it all costs. I guess she's glad we have lots left over to take home. She even agrees to drive back to the farm after dinner, so Dulcy and I can go swimming.

I wait at Parker Pool all afternoon, but Jeff Tan never shows up.

19

I SHOULD FEEL ELATED ABOUT WINNING AT HIGH JUMP. But instead I feel depressed all the way back to the farm. My heart and mind are full of visions of Clare lying in her hospital bed. How things will turn out for her seems way more important than how things worked out for me at the track meet.

Sure, I did it. I jumped higher than Arden Hampton-Price. And I made 1.45, a personal best.

But so what?

There's no glow.

No glory.

The joy jumping always gives me isn't there anymore. And I'm afraid it's gone forever.

*

But when we get back from the farm, Grandma greets us with good news. Clare woke up for about half an hour today. Right around the time I was jumping. How cool is that?

Clare even talked a bit to Aunt Faye. The first word Clare said was, "Mom?" And the next was, "Renzo?"

And then Aunt Faye had to tell Clare about the accident and her surgery and everything. Which must have been hard.

But Clare wanted to know — she didn't want to be spared any details. Apparently the last thing she said before she closed her eyes and slipped back into her sedated state again was, "I'll be okay."

As I try to fall asleep, I overhear my parents talking as they sit out in the rocking chairs on the verandah.

"Thank heavens Clare's coming around now that they don't have to keep her so heavily sedated," Mom says. "And wasn't Morgan great? Wow, what a day."

"Right," Dad says. "I'm pretty proud of Morgan. But Clare — there's still such a long way to go. They won't be cutting back on her pain killers for a while, so there's still the addiction problem."

"I know it's not going to be easy," Mom says. "But I feel a whole lot more hopeful. I just wish it wasn't such a strain for Faye, driving back and forth, and trying to keep up with things at home too."

"And if the doctors decide to send Clare to a rehab facility," Dad says, "that's going to be even more driving."

"Faye wants to bring her home," Mom says. "Even if it is more work. And you know, if it was me, I'd feel the same. I'd want my daughter home."

She would?

"There's a lesson in this," Mom continues.

I groan and punch at my pillow. Trust Mom to turn everything into a learning situation.

"For me, at least," Mom says, "it's made me realize what an awful lot of time and energy people waste on things that don't really matter."

"Mmmhhhmmm," Dad says into the sound of the rocking chairs.

"I shouldn't have made Morgan spend the summer here."

I get up and creep right over to the window.

"I was so sure it would be good for her to get away from Jade," Mom says. "I wanted her to have the farm, the fields, the fresh air — just like I had."

Dad doesn't answer.

For a few minutes all I can hear is the steady creaking of the rocking chairs. Then Mom's voice again. "Jim, I want Morgan home for the rest of the summer. I ... I ... well, I want her with me."

Silence. Even the rocking stops. "Jim?" No answer. "Jim? What do you think?"

Then I hear something that sounds like a snore.

"Fine," Mom says. "That's settled then. Morgan will be coming home with us."

*

I sleep in the next morning. Everyone else is up and dressed by the time I come downstairs. "Sweetheart!" Mom throws her arms around me. "Honey, guess what?"

As I hug her I realize how much I've missed her physical presence. Her arms feel so solid and strong around me. "What, Mom?"

"You're coming back home with us today."

"I am?" I try to act surprised, even though I've had hours to think about it. "But what about the hospital and all?"

Mom pours me some orange juice. "We'll make a trip to see Clare on the way home."

"I'm not coming home," Glen says. "You can't make me. I'm going back to camp."

"It's okay, Glen," Dad says. "We know that."

"Thanks Mom," I say. "But I, well, it means a lot that you want me back. And I *do* miss you, but if you don't mind, I'd really rather stay here."

"You would? But I thought, I mean, you said you wanted to come home so many times, and we can do up your room —"

"I did want to come home, at first. Well, right up until yesterday, actually. But I've changed my mind. My room can wait, everything in Northington can wait. Aunt Faye needs a lot of help right now."

"Oh." Mom sits down at the table and rests her head in her hands.

"While Clare's in hospital I can help Aunt Faye with all the cooking and cleaning, and I can hang out with Dulcy. I could even help out around the farm. And then when Clare comes home I can help with her physio exercises and all that."

"Oh," Mom says again.

"Till school starts, okay?"

Mom looks at me with an expression both happy and sad. "Okay. And Morgan? I'm proud of you." She pokes at Dad, who is sitting beside her devouring his breakfast. "What do you say, Jim?"

"Yum." Dad smiles as he bites into one of the fresh blueberry muffins Grandma baked.

"Oh, and by the way," I say to Glen, who is also gobbling down a muffin. "If you're ever lost in a cornfield, just follow a row. Sooner or later you'll come to the edge."

"Yeah?" Glen says. "Thanks, I'll remember that. Hey, could you pass the milk?"

*

That night I lie awake again, thinking up another plan. A plan to get over Seraphina and the hold she's had on us. Because I've figured out that by keeping her story alive, Grandma's kept the grief alive too. I know she told me she moved on when she got married, but I think she's got a ways to go yet. Instead of happy memories of her sister, she has unhappy memories of Seraphina's death.

After breakfast I watch my parents and Glen leave, wondering how I'll get along without Mom. But now that I'm speaking to her again, I can call her whenever I want. And she and Dad will be out some weekends to see me and Clare.

When the car is out of sight, I go inside and call Dulcy to come right over.

Then I ask Grandma, who's sitting at the table reading the newspaper, "Can we have Seraphina's hair?"

Grandma sets down her tea cup and looks shocked. "Whatever for?"

"Because I was thinking about it all night, and you know what? It's time to let her go."

"Oh," Grandma says. "Well, I — "

"The hair, Gram," I say, opening the sideboard drawer. "Please?"

She folds her newspaper and comes over to where I'm holding the box of Seraphina's hair. I open it and say, "You can have one last look."

Grandma touches the hair and sighs. "I suppose you're right," she says. "Sixty-one years is long enough. I'll trust you with this, Morgan. Don't tell me why you want it, just take it."

So I do.

When Dulcy arrives we unbraid the grass around Seraphina's Circle, brushing it out in waves. Then we go in. Along with the box of Seraphina's hair, I've brought a garden trowel. I start digging by the Clare and Renzo dolls' living room. "Go get some flowers, Dulcy."

"What are we doing?"

"You'll see."

Dulcy watches me dig for a few minutes. Finally she says, "Okay, I guess."

While she's gone I scoop a hole beside the dolls' living room. When Dulcy comes back she has a huge bouquet of phlox, black-eyed Susans and Queen Anne's lace.

"Now we have to bury Seraphina's buckle and her hair," I say, "right here in Seraphina's Circle."

"We do?" Dulcy says, fiddling with the flowers.

"We do." I place the box of hair in the ground and put the tarnished butterfly buckle on top. "In memory of Seraphina," I say.

"May she rest in peace," Dulcy says.

"And may this be the end of her story."

Then we fill in the hole with sandy soil and pine needles, patting everything down smoothly. We heap the flowers on top, making it look like a grave. My hands get all dusty and I wipe them on my shorts, patting the pocket where I kept that buckle. I feel lighter already.

When we're finished, Dulcy rubs the sweat off her forehead. Her hand leaves a dirty smudge. "Now what?" She looks around Seraphina's Circle like she's lost.

I wipe off her face with my sleeve. "Want to make the new dolls now?"

"Dunno," Dulcy says. "I don't feel like playing with them anymore."

"Yeah, me either."

"Could we high jump?"

I remember winning at the all-star track meet and then the awful letdown feeling after. *No!* I want to scream. *I'm never high jumping again.* But what I hear myself say is, "Okay. It's time you started learning the flop. And I want to clear 1.5 next year."

"But Morgan? I forgot your pole's broken."

"No problem. We can fix it — Grandma's got duct tape."

The duct tape works — sort of. The pole isn't solid anymore and it sags in the middle. But even though it's wonky, it's good enough.

As we jump, I pretend to be having fun so Dulcy will feel better. I try to forget about myself and concentrate on teaching her the flop. She tries really hard, so hard that I have to keep helping her.

We practise for the rest of the morning. And after a while, the pure, free joy I thought would never come again begins tugging at my heart. It doesn't overwhelm me. But it hints at the possibility. And it glimmers with the hope that someday, if I keep trying, I'll be able to clear anything.

OTHER BOOKS BY JOCELYN SHIPLEY

GETTING A LIFE

Fifteen-year-old Carly is struggling to handle the increasing complexities of her life — homework, hanging out with the in crowd at school and parents who don't seem to understand her point of view. Tough-talking Dawn Radford has just moved in across the street and seems to have everything Carly doesn't: glamour, style and the confidence to deal with boys. Though her effort to befriend the Radfords ends disastrously, Carly gradually learns to look beyond appearances and to take charge of her own life.

"... Carly's dilemmas are ... universal, and her vivid, three-dimensional personality is captivating. ...she leaps off the page, holding readers' attention until her struggle to come to grips with herself comes to a promising close."
— *School Library Journal*

"... fresh and true ... hard to put down."
— *CM Magazine*
**** Highly Recommended

CROSS MY HEART

The youngest of three sisters, Jill Summerfield is growing up in south-western Ontario in the turbulent decade of the Sixties. Her oldest sister is way too perfect; her middle sister is eccentric and dreamy. As the world around her changes, Jill moves from square to cool, from Bobby Vinton to the Beatles, and from cowgirl suits to push-up bras. In these linked stories of friendship and betrayal, *Cross My Heart* offers a vivid portrayal of the timeless passions and stresses of growing up female.

"... true to life and honest."　　— *CM Magazine*
**** Highly Recommended

"... a true-to-life portrayal of the universal struggles of growing up, which readers will easily relate to."
— *Canadian Children's Book News*

Other Books for Young Adults from Sumach Press ...

Find out more at www.sumachpress.com